The Adventures of Captain Hex by Edgar Wallace

Richard Horatio Edgar Wallace was born on the 1st April 1875 in Greenwich, London. Leaving school at 12 because of truancy, by the age of fifteen he had experience; selling newspapers, as a worker in a rubber factory, as a shoe shop assistant, as a milk delivery boy and as a ship's cook.

By 1894 he was engaged but broke it off to join the Infantry being posted to South Africa. He also changed his name to Edgar Wallace which he took from Lew Wallace, the author of Ben-Hur.

In Cape Town in 1898 he met Rudyard Kipling and was inspired to begin writing. His first collection of ballads, The Mission that Failed! was enough of a success that in 1899 he paid his way out of the armed forces in order to turn to writing full time.

By 1904 he had completed his first thriller, The Four Just Men. Since nobody would publish it he resorted to setting up his own publishing company which he called Tallis Press.

In 1911 his Congolese stories were published in a collection called Sanders of the River, which became a bestseller. He also started his own racing papers, Bibury's and R. E. Walton's Weekly, eventually buying his own racehorses and losing thousands gambling. A life of exceptionally high income was also mirrored with exceptionally large spending and debts.

Wallace now began to take his career as a fiction writer more seriously, signing with Hodder and Stoughton in 1921. He was marketed as the 'King of Thrillers' and they gave him the trademark image of a trilby, a cigarette holder and a yellow Rolls Royce. He was truly prolific, capable not only of producing a 70,000 word novel in three days but of doing three novels in a row in such a manner. It was estimated that by 1928 one in four books being read was written by Wallace, for alongside his famous thrillers he wrote variously in other genres, including science fiction, non-fiction accounts of WWI which amounted to ten volumes and screen plays. Eventually he would reach the remarkable total of 170 novels, 18 stage plays and 957 short stories.

Wallace became chairman of the Press Club which to this day holds an annual Edgar Wallace Award, rewarding 'excellence in writing'.

Diagnosed with diabetes his health deteriorated and he soon entered a coma and died of his condition and double pneumonia on the 7th of February 1932 in North Maple Drive, Beverly Hills. He was buried near his home in England at Chalklands, Bourne End, in Buckinghamshire.

Index of Contents

CHAPTER I

MR. MONTAGUE FLAKE, THE MARGARINE KING, HANDS OVER £8,000

Captain Reggie Hex threw up the window of his sitting-room and looked across the chimney tops of Bloomsbury with a critical eye.

It was a sunny day, and even chimney-tops and untidy back-windows have a poetry in the golden light of an early morning in summer to a young man plentifully endowed with faith in his own capabilities.

His age may have been twenty-six, and he was passably good-looking. He had a pair of bright, blue, humourous eyes that seemed forever laughing, a straight nose, a firm, large mouth, shaded by the smallest of moustaches.

His face was tanned brick-red, and he had the appearance of being what in fact he was—an army officer in mufti. If you looked twice at him you realised that the mufti was shabby, and when he turned round, so that the slanting sunlight caught his garments in a searching light, the suggestion of poverty became more apparent.

When he walked to the table which had been laid for him it was noticeable that he limped slightly, and if this minor infirmity be compared with the evidence of the silver badge in the lapel of his coat and the framed certificate above the writing-table in one corner of the room the cause and effect were exposed.

The room was sparsely furnished. Green felt covered the floor, a plain green paper the walls. There was an old gate-legged table, two or three rush-bottom chairs, a big lounge chair which Captain Hex had alone salvaged from the wreckage of his civilian possessions, and the writing-table made up the furniture.

There were a few cheap prints of old masters scattered about the room, a few framed photographs on the mantelpiece, and the only remarkable decoration of the chamber was that which filled the greater portion on one wall space.

It was formed by two great sheets of brown paper. On the surface were neatly pasted at intervals photographs which had evidently been cut from illustrated newspapers.

Captain Hex's "Man Friday"

"Belshazzar Smith," he called imperiously.

"Sir," said a muffled voice.

"Bring your grub in here."

"Harf a mo', sir," said the voice. "I'll get my coat on."

In a few moments there appeared, a plate in one hand and a cup in the other, Belshazzar Smith, late private of the Scots Guards, six feet high, and broad; a sandy man of gentle countenance, with a little ginger moustache and shaggy eyebrows that topped a pair of solemn blue eyes. Add to this a certain baldness and you have the man. He had this in common with his master—that he wore in the button-hole of his ill-fitting coat the silver badge of service.

"Sit down, Belshazzar Smith," said Captain Hex, reaching out and drawing a chair to the table. "We'll start fair."

"I'd just as soon have my grub in the kitchen if you don't mind, sir," pleaded the soldier.

"Be a democrat," snarled Hex. "Sit down with your equals and even worse—where the devil did you get that name of Belshazzar?"

"A Bible name, sir," said Mr. Smith with great gravity. "All our family had that kind of name: Abijah, Shallum, Jotham, Pekah, and Gehazi."

"Good Lord!" said the startled Captain Hex. "You had a lucky escape, for if Belshazzar is a Biblical name, I'm a Hun. But let that go. We will review the situation. I met you last night for the first time!"

"Yes, sir."

"You were broke."

"Yes, sir."

"I offered you a job at nothing a week, but with prospects."

"Yes, sir."

"Go on eating, Belshazzar. You're discharged from the army. Why don't you go back to your old job?"

Mr. Smith was silent.

"Because," Captain Hex went on, "because there is no old job—that's what you told me last night. Because you left a little shop to join the army and when you came out you found it in the hands of a healthy young alien named—"

"Livinski," growled Mr. Smith, bolting his toast savagely. "He's opened three shops—all belonging to men who were called up. As Shakespeare says—"

"Blow Shakespeare!" said Captain Hex. "Now listen to me. I had a business in 1914. It was a good business—foreign agency, stock-buying, and all that sort of thing. I chucked it up: two thousand a year, closed my office, and went into the army.

"Today," he said grimly, "every one of my customers is on the books of Rosenbaum and Toblinsky. From their names," he went on, "you might imagine that they are Irish [sic]. "They're not. They're Russians. They are rich, Belshazzar, rich beyond the dreams of actresses."

"Avarice," murmured Belshazzar Smith, on familiar ground.

"Actresses," insisted Captain Hex firmly, "come here."

He rose and walked to the wall, where his picture-gallery offended the unities and stabbed with his finger portrait after portrait, as he reeled off their titles and biographies.

"That's William O. McNeal, real name Adolph Bernsteiner, the Shell King; that is Harry V. Teckle, the Steel King; that is Theodore Match, the Shipping King; that is Montague G. Flake, the Margarine King; this fellow with the funny nose is Michael O. Blogg, the Jam King—and that fellow with the glasses is the Cotton King; and that lad with the dyspeptic eye and the diamond pin is the Lumber King—bow to Their Majesties, Belshazzar Smith. They are going to make us rich!"

"Sir?" said the startled and baffled Mr. Smith.

"They are our little Eldorados," said Captain Hex calmly, "our Pay Cash or Bearers; our Money from Home!"

"Do you mean they're relations of yours?" Said Belshazzar, in tones of awe.

"God forbid!" said Captain Hex piously. "Sit you down and I'll expound the Plan of Operations and the General Idea."

For an hour he expounded his scheme, and comprehension came very slowly to Mr. Smith, but it came.

"And now," said Captain Hex, getting up, "we will go to the office, and the great advantage of living in your office, Smith, is that you aren't very far from home."

He walked to the writing-table, pulled open a drawer, and took out a wad of press-cuttings, and from these he selected one.

"Before we proceed," he said, "go down to the front door and hang out the board. You will find it in the kitchen. We must do everything regularly.

Mr. Smith disappeared into the tiny kitchen, and presently returned with a small black board on which was painted in white letters—

HEX'S DETECTIVE AGENCY
(Restitution Department)

"That's right," said Hex approvingly. "You will find two nails outside the door, and your job will be to hang it out every morning and take it in every night, providing the youth of Lambeth does not pinch it."

When Smith returned, his employer took up the cutting.

"Listen to this. It is a description of a sale at Christie's. 'A small box of miscellaneous manuscript went to the bid of Mr. Montague Flake at 120 guineas. The box is of carved Spanish mahogany,' etc., etc. I will not bother you with the details. The point is that Mr. Flake is a great collector of old manuscript and a great hog."

"Now, your part is dead easy," continued Captain Hex, consulting a Bradshaw. "You go down to—let me see—yes, here is a likely place called Little Wenson, and buy a farm. Do the best you can with £200, but remember, it has got to be a free-hold property. It need not be large. It need not be near a road, and preferably there should be at least one tree."

"I am to buy it?" said Mr. Smith slowly.

That is your job," Hex said. "You can take your time. Live as cheaply as you can, but don't close the deal until you get a wire from me. Send me all the particulars, a rough sketch of the property, and your address. You are not to communicate with me except through this office, and under no circumstances are you to disclose the fact that you know me or have any business dealings with me."

An hour later Smith left. Captain Hex took off his coat and set to work. In a box in his bedroom were half-a-dozen sheets of age-stained parchment. He spent the rest of the morning and the greater part of the afternoon covering these with fine writing.

There is no more highly respected figure in financial and business circles than Mr. Montague Flake, for Mr. Flake controlled the butter markets of London, Copenhagen, Rotterdam and, in pre-war days, Tomsk, from which it may be gathered that Mr. Flake was a considerable personage even before the time he managed to corner the butter supplies.

Officially, Mr. Flake did not control the market. Officially he had nothing to do with the cornering of margarine. In all his stores—and there were 631 branches of Flake U.P. Stores throughout the United Kingdom—the "U.P." standing for "Universal Provisions"—there was a large notice respectfully informing customers that the management was doing its best to get supplies of butter and margarine, but that the failure of the hay crop in Denmark, and the root crop in Ireland, was causing much embarrassment, whilst the extra cost of freights (which really worked out at an additional ¼d per pound), compelled the reluctant directors to raise the price of butter 3d per pound, and margarine 2½d.

And the customers were duly impressed, and, what is more to the point, they paid, and millions of twopence-ha'pennies went into Mr. Flake's pocket, for he was the company, the directors and the shareholders. This was in the days when the price of butter was not controlled and when butter-cards were unknown.

Mr. Flake had a large house in St John's Square, in the most fashionable part of London. He had a model farm in Norfolk, an estate in Kent, a shoot in Yorkshire and a salmon river in Scotland.

Mr. Flake was a harsh-faced man, wholly unsuggestive of butter or anything oleaginous or suave. He was a widower and lived alone, save a housekeeper, three secretaries, four chauffeurs, twelve men-servants, and a small army of white-capped cooks, housemaids, and the like.

Mr. Flake sat in his magnificent library, and was nibbling his pen, for he was in the agony of composition.

He had scratched out twenty lines when a visitor was announced. He took up the card that lay on the silver plate and read the inscription without any great show of interest. It read:

THE HEX PRIVATE DETECTIVE AGENCY
(Restitution Department)
Captain Reginald Hex, D.S.O., M.C.,
late Blitheshire Fusiliers

He glared up at his secretary, who had followed the footman into the room.

"What does he want? Tell him to write."

"He insists upon seeing you, sir," said the footman. "I told him you were busy."

"Show him in," growled Mr. Flake.

Captain Hex was ushered in, very grave, very business-like and very well dressed, for he wore his one good suit.

"Sit down. Captain—er—Hex," said Mr. Flake, waving his lordly hand to a chair. "What can I do for you?"

Captain Hex removed his gloves slowly, laid them beside his hat, took out his pocket-book and consulted the interior.

"A few days ago," he said, "you purchased a number of miscellaneous manuscripts at Christie's sale."

Mr. Flake nodded.

"They were the property," Captain Hex went on, "of the late Lord Witherall, who was a collector, and they comprised a number of more or less important documents—"

"More or less worthless," interrupted Mr. Flake brusquely. "As a matter of fact, I bought that lot for the box more than for the manuscripts. I haven't had time to look through them yet, but I don't suppose the manuscripts are worth tuppence."

"It was on the subject of the manuscripts I wanted to see you," said Hex. "I have been employed by a client to interview you under peculiar circumstances. A former confidential servant of Lord Witherall gave into his lordship's custody certain documents, the particulars of which I am not at liberty to give, and these, according to the man's relatives—he has been dead some years, by the way—were kept by his lordship in that particular box. The man's name was Samuels, though that was not the name he was known by to Lord Witherall. If that document is in your possession—it is in the form of a letter addressed to Samuels—my client is willing to pay you £200 for its return."

Now Mr. Flake was, above all things, a good business man, and a good business man knows instinctively that a first offer of £200 for anything means that it is worth much more. And a good business man, moreover, has ever an eye to the main chance.

Mr. Flake pressed a bell, and, when his secretary appeared:—

"Bring me that box I bought at Christie's the other day," he said. "I can tell you this," he said, when the girl had gone, "that I do not promise that I can return any document which may be in this box. A deal's a deal. Captain Hex, and I am a business man."

Captain Hex nodded.

"I can only remind you," he said gently, "that the relatives of Samuels are very poor people, and from what I gather that document may be of the greatest value to them."

"And to me," said Mr. Flake pleasantly. "I am poor, too. We are all poor—it is a relative term, as we are on the subject of relatives," he added humorously.

"I don't think you can compare your condition with theirs, sir," said Captain Hex with dignity, "and I feel sure that you would not attempt to benefit at the expense of poor people—"

"Rubbish!" snapped Montague Flake. "There is no sentiment in my composition, Captain Hex. I am a self-made man, and I have made my money without worrying very much about the people who have had to part. A bargain is a bargain. If I pay 120 guineas for a poke, I'm entitled to the pig I find in it. That's fair, ain't it—isn't it, I mean? Mind you, I'm not going to say I won't sell it," he added, as the secretary placed the box on the big table before him, "and I'm not going to say I will."

He cut the sealed cords which bound the box, and threw open the lid. It was filled to the top with yellow manuscripts. Some were bound together in pads with faded red ribbon. some were bound together in vellum books, and there were a large number of loose sheets.

Mr. Flake hesitated and, lifting out the first stratum, laid it on the desk.

"You say it is a letter?" he said.

Captain Hex nodded.

"This is evidently the manuscript of an old play," said Mr. Flake; "and this"—he lifted another weighty pile—"seems to be the original manuscript of a story of some kind. Here are the letters." He picked one up, turned it over to read the signature, and laid it on the table.

Hex turned to the waiting secretary, and then to Mr. Flake with an air of indecision.

"I wonder if your secretary would be good enough to look up the telephone number of Sir John Howard and Sons."

He named the greatest of the London solicitors, a name which carried respect even to Mr. Flake.

"Are you acting for Howard?" he asked quickly.

"For the moment I cannot disclose my principals," he said.

He looked round and waited until the door closed behind the girl; then he sidled close to Mr. Flake.

"I can tell you this in confidence," he said in a low voice. I am acting for—"

He whispered a name in Mr. Flake's ear. To reach the financier he had to come round to the corner of the table. As he whispered, he obscured for a moment Mr. Flake's view of the box. With somebody whispering in your ear, it is difficult to detect the rustle of parchment.

Hex's hand shot into the open box, and was out again before Mr. Flake could recover from his surprise.

"Tup?" said Mr. Flake irritably. "Who the dickens is Tup?"

"That," said the suave Captain Hex, "I will reveal at some later stage of the enquiry. I thought you knew."

Mr. Flake looked at him searchingly, but the eyes of Captain Hex did not falter.

"Anyway," said the financier, as he bundled the documents back into the box, "I haven't time to go through these things now, and I shan't be able to give you an answer for a few days."

"But it is urgent." Captain Hex was earnest again. "If it is a question of money we shall not quarrel over a few hundreds. It is absolutely necessary that we should get this document back immediately."

"And it is absolutely necessary," said Mr. Flake good-humouredly, "that I should have my afternoon tea and that I should have time to examine the contents. I will give you your answer tomorrow."

With this Captain Hex had to be content. He left the house, curiously enough, without discovering the telephone number he had inquired for, and made his way to the nearest post office. He sent a telegram addressed to "Smith, Bull Hotel, Little Wenson, Kent," and the message was: "Close the deal."

Four days later a handsome motor-car drew up before a very small cottage a mile from the village of Little Wenson, and Mr. Flake descended.

Fortunately, he was able to make his reconnaissance without effort, for the cottage stood at the corner of a lane and the western limit of the garden ran flush with the hedge. There were two apple trees, and beyond the broken wall of a well with its crazy windlass.

Mr. Flake walked slowly back to the front of the cottage, pushed open the gate, walked along the garden path and knocked at the door. A man in his shirt sleeves answered: a tall, solemn-looking man, who answered Mr. Flake's cheery "Good morning!" with a non-committal nod.

"Is this your house?" asked Mr. Flake pleasantly.

"Yes, sir," said the cottager.

"Rather nice situation," said Mr. Flake.

"It's not so bad," said the other, cautiously.

"Been here long?"

"About a week," said the occupant. "I haven't been out of the army long, and I thought of starting a poultry farm."

"Oh, so you were in the army?" said Mr. Flake, patronisingly. "Well, it doesn't seem the right kind of place to raise chickens. Who owned it before you?"

"I forget the name," said the cottager, "but it's been in the same family for hundreds of years."

"H'm!" said Mr. Flake. Then, carelessly: "Can't you recall the name?"

"Something like Samson," said the cottager, with an effort of memory.

"Was it Samuels?" asked Mr. Flake, eagerly.

"Ah, that's the name, Samuels. They weren't the last tenants, but they were the people who owned it years ago."

"H'm!" said Mr. Flake again. "If it isn't asking you a rude question, what did you pay for it?"

"All the money I had," parried the other skilfully, "and as Publius Syrus says—"

"Yes, yes," said Mr. Flake. I know what the public say. But now, tell me—what would you sell this little property for?"

"I wouldn't sell it," said the cottager.

"Come, come, you'd sell it for £100 profit, surely?" said Mr. Flake.

"Not for £1,000 profit," said the other, determinedly. "Not for £10,000 profit. There's some funny tales going about this property. I had a lawyer down here the other day and a private detective."

"The devil you did!" said Mr. Flake. "Come, now, let's talk business. I am a business man, and I will give you £1,000 for this property."

"If you offered me £20,000 I wouldn't take it," said the cottager, with greater determination than ever. "I am satisfied with it, and, as Socrates says: 'Contentment is natural wealth; luxury is artificial poverty.'"

"Now look here" Mr. Flake was aroused. "Will you take a reasonable price for this property? I've got a fancy for it, and I will pay anything in reason."

"Come inside," said the cottager, opening the door. 'Wise men are instructed by reason,' says Cicero; 'men of lesser understanding by experience.'"

An hour later Mr. Smith shook the dust of Little Wenson from his feet. He was accompanied to London by Mr. Flake, and together they journeyed to a bank in Lombard Street, for Mr. Smith admitted to a wholesome horror of cheques, and not until he had received pads of large white banknotes did he affix his signature to the deed which transferred his property to Mr. Flake.

It was a long time since Mr. Flake had done a day's hard digging, but he felt that he was being well repaid for his labours when, at six o'clock the next morning, he began his excavations. A line drawn at right angles from the centre of the two apple trees passed the well on the right hand side. This was exactly as the document in his possession said it should pass.

Those three sheets of parchment written in a crabbed hand describing how one William Samuels had in the year 1826 stolen from the strong rooms of Cheals Bank, at which he was employed as a porter, "brilliant stones to the value of £120,000, the property of the French emigré, the Marquis du Thierry," and of how he had hidden that same in the garden of brother-in-law, Henry Frederick Samuels, in the parish of Little Wenson, were consulted again and again.

The said box was there. A perspiring Mr. Flake discovered it after three hours' strenuous digging and brought it to the light. It looked strangely new. Indeed an ordinary person might have confused it with one of those solid boxes which farmers employ to send eggs by rail. It was heavy, but Mr. Flake did not feel its weight as he carried it to the seclusion of the cottage and prized off its top.

It was heavy because it was half-filled with sand. He ran his hand through the sand, and his fingers encountered a square piece of cardboard, which he took out and carried to the light, for he was a near-sighted.

There was one line of writing, and that in the same crabbed calligraphy as the letter he had found in his box of manuscript—though, if he had examined that box before Captain Hex had whispered in his ear, he might have saved himself a great deal of labour and no small amount of money.

The inscription ran:

TUP means The Unfortunate People, on whose behalf I am acting.

The next morning Mr. Flake waited upon Captain Hex. "You and your gang have swindled me out of £8,000," he said. "You can either hand the money back or be prosecuted."

"Thank you very kindly," said Captain Hex. "I will be prosecuted."

"You are a common swindler," stormed Mr. Flake.

"There are two ways out of this room," said Captain Hex. "One is out of the window and one is out of the door. You have paid your money, so you can take your choice."

"I shall go to the police," fumed Mr. Flake, taking up his hat.

He was on the point of apoplexy.

"Now listen to me," said Captain Hex kindly. "You got the worst of a deal. You thought you were going to make a lot of money at the expense of a poor family. You have spent your life getting fat on the money you have twisted from the public. The war has been a godsend for you. That you should get rich and have your shooting boxes and your country estates, soldiers' wives and soldiers' children have gone hungry. The law cannot touch you. You are one of the thieves who keep within the law. I have taken £8,000 from you on a square deal, and I tell you this"—he shook his finger in the purple face of the speechless financier—"that £8,000 will be £80,000 before I have done with you."

"You are a common thief!" spluttered Mr. Flake.

"Belshazzar Smith," called Hex sternly, and the big man appeared in the doorway, "chuck this blighter out."

Belshazzar opened the door and jerked his thumb.

"As 'Azlitt says—'Violence defeats its own ends.'"

What else Hazlitt said, Mr. Flake did not wait to hear.

CHAPTER II

THE OUTWITTING OF MR. THEODORE MATCH

"Belshazzar Smith," said Captain Hex suddenly.

They had sat for an hour in the fading light, smoking in silence. The evening sky was still light, and through the open window came the shrill voices of children at play.

"Sir?" said Belshazzar Smith.

"Light the gas and have a look at the picture gallery."

Belshazzar Smith rose heavily, put his big pipe on the mantelshelf, and lit the gas. The he walked across to the wall on which were pasted a number of portraits cut from the illustrated papers.

"In the second row, the third from the right, you find—what?"

"Theodore Match," read Mr. Smith.

"That's the man. Well, Theodore Match, Esquire, who has never given a ha'penny to charity, is going to provide a start in life for some fifty soldiers' families."

Mr. Smith nodded and reached for his pipe.

"That's better," he said. "As Fielding says, 'A rich man without charity is a rogue,' and, as 'Errick says—"

"We'll leave 'Errick out," said Captain Hex. "Anyway, you needn't praise Mr. Match. He'll be Sir Theodore Match in the next Honours List, because he doesn't know how generous he is going to be. Belshazzar, is your tobacco dearer than it used to be? Is meat dearer—is bread dearer—is everything dearer that comes from overseas? Who do you think has got the extra ha'pence? The planter and the farmer have got a bit. They worked for it and good luck to them. But Theodore Match has got more than his whack. He's had a ha'penny of yours for tobacco and a farthing for your loaf of bread and something out of everything you eat or drink. He's raised his freights. Coal is dear, labour is dearer—everything's dear. But he's the dearest thing of all. There's nothing cheap about Theodore except the souls he sends to sea and the men he employs and his patriotic speeches. I have put him down on the subscription list to my Cottage Homes for the Widows and Orphans of the Mercantile Marine for the sum of £8,000—and I'll get it."

Mr. Smith nodded slowly, and there was admiration in his eyes.

"I bet you will, sir," he said enthusiastically.

The Theodore Steamship Line, as everybody knows, is one of the most important cargo lines in the United Kingdom. It had a fleet of 25 ships, it traded with South America, with the China seas and with the two coasts, and with India and Africa, and before the war did an extensive business between West Africa and Hamburg.

Its head offices were in Newcastle; and to Newcastle Captain Hex, accompanied by his trusty lieutenant, journeyed next day, arriving late in the evening and repairing at once to the Station Hotel.

Early in the morning Captain Hex set forth on a voyage of discovery. The Theodore Steamship Line possessed an unpretentious block of offices not very far from the hotel, and by the energy of the clerks and the number of clients who waited in the various departments, Hex gathered that business was extensively brisk.

He passed into the office, handed his card to a clerk and presently was shown into the private room of Mr. Theodore Match. It was a large room, half-panelled in oak and hung about with photographs of ships. Mr. Match was a middle-aged man with one of those jovial, bearded countenances and those easily laughing eyes which are the possession of men upon whom the cares and worries of this world sit lightly.

He beamed at his visitor through gold-rimmed glasses.

"Glad to meet you, Captain Hex," he said, to that officer's surprise. "Sit you down and make yourself comfortable. Have a cigar."

He handed a silver box to the visitor and Hex slowly selected a weed.

"Now what is it you want?" smiled Mr. Match. "£10,000 for a soldier's model farm or a million to found an asylum for worn-out quartermasters?"

For a second, but only for a second. Hex was surprised to silence.

"I think I'll take the million," he said, "though, as a matter of fact, I don't want anything like that sum."

Mr. Match leant back in his chair, shaking with laughter and rubbing his hands together as though he were a participant in the greatest joke in the world.

"You see, I know you, Captain Hex. As a matter of fact, I've been warned about you. I'll tell you frankly, I know all about your little office in Hope Street, Lambeth. I know all about your portrait gallery—I sent a private detective there the other day to have a look round—I know all about your adventures with Mr. Montague Flake, who is an old friend and client of ours. I know how you diddled him out of £8,000. I've been laughing over that ever since. Now let us come down to plain speaking, MCaptain Hex," he said, leaning forward and resting his elbows on the arms of his chair. "You imagine you have a mission in life to relieve rich men of their unearned surpluses. Am I right?"

Hex was now at his ease. He recognised the situation and his mind was working rapidly.

"That is perfectly true," he said. "I have."

"Good!" said Mr. Match heartily. "You have marked down a dozen disgustingly rich people to contribute the soldiers' and sailors' comfort."

"That also is true," said Hex.

"Good again!" said Mr. Match. "You regard me as a profiteer and you have come to Newcastle with a grand little scheme in your head to make me contribute to—what?"

"I have been settling soldiers on the land," said Hex. "I want to provide a few homes for wives and children of the men of the Mercantile Marine."

"Admirable philanthropist!"

The eyes of Mr. Theodore Match were beaming with benevolent fun. He stroked his little beard thoughtfully.

"Admirable philanthropist!" he repeated. "And how much am I supposed to contribute to this very interesting experiment of yours?"

"I have put you down for £8,000," said Hex.

"Why not £8,000,000? I am as willing to give one as the other. And I suppose you have some little scheme to get it. Now be a sportsman, Captain Hex," he said banteringly. "What shall it be? A grand confidence trick, buried treasure, interesting details about my past life. You won't enlighten me as to the little trick you intended employing to extract my hard-won wealth?"

Hex laughed.

"I will give you frankness for frankness," he said. "I hadn't quite made up my mind."

"Come," said the other, "be friendly."

The door opened at that moment and a young man came in, a tall, stout-built young man, red and puffy of face.

"This is my son; this is Captain Hex, about whom I was speaking to you, Tom," said Theodore Match. "You will be interested to learn, Captain Hex, and it will probably add to your righteous anger against the profiteer, than my son is 27, unmarried, perfectly fit so far as I know, but so indispensable to my business that he was exempted. That's so, Tom, isn't it?"

Tom grinned.

"That's about the size of it," he said.

"Of course," said Mr. Match, still smiling, "he ought to have been in the cold, damp trenches of Flanders from your point of view, instead of being in a warm, snug flat in Newcastle. Now, come, Captain Hex, "have I not tempted you to do your uttermost."

"Tell me, before we go any farther," said Hex, "will you contribute anything to my scheme?"

"Not a bean," smiled the other, "not half a bean, not the very dust that lies at the bottom of a bag of beans. Why should I? Am I sitting here making money for my servants or for myself? Do I devote the whole of my day and the greater part of my night to working out schemes for increasing my super-tax in order to bring trade and custom to a hundred local public-houses? No, sir!" He thumped his desk furiously. "The welfare of my men does not interest me. What they do with their money does not interest me either. What I do with my own is no concern of theirs or yours or anybody else's in the world."

"Do you want me, governor?" asked the young man.

"No, Tom, I merely wanted you to come in to see Captain Hex."

With a nod to the visitor and a meaning grin to his parent Tom Match left the room.

"I make more money than the able seaman because I am cleverer than the able seaman," continued Mr. Match. "It is the triumph of intellect over brute strength. Show me anybody who is cleverer than I and let him take it out of me, and I am perfectly willing that he shall get away with it. If you"—he pointed a pencil at Hex and spoke more slowly—"or your military attaché, who I understand bears the uncommon name of Smith, can by any trick or dodge or act of artfulness, short of forgery or burglary or robbery, extract from, me £8,000 or £10,000, you are at liberty to do so.

"I tell you this frankly, and as man to man, Captain Hex, that the welfare of the seaman is of no interest to me. I am ever so much more interested in you, and if you can find a way of getting the better of me, if you can trap me in a unguarded moment by any trick you may choose into giving you the money you require, I promise you that I will not prosecute you even though the act by which you extract the money may be a criminal one in the eyes of the law."

He stood up, still smiling, and thrust out his big hand, and Hex was smiling as he gripped it. There was something about this Philistine that he liked. If he were a brute, he was an honest brute.

"I accept your challenge," he said. "Within a week you will have contributed £8.000 to an unexpected charity."

"You can't do it," said Mr. Match decidedly. "Why, my dear man, I have successfully resisted an appeal of the highest people in the land. Look here!"

He walked back to his desk, pulled open a drawer and flung out half a dozen printed documents, attached by a fastener.

"It came this morning—the Prince's Appeal for Merchant Seamen. That's one better than yours. They want a million," he chuckled. "Did I refuse it? No, sir, I ignored it. If I refused I should get into bad odour—you realize we are speaking in confidence as men of honour. If the Prince comes to Newcastle I shall dodge him. If he writes me a personal letter I shall be on a bed of sickness and unable to reply. I have never given a ha'porth of charity in my life and, please heaven, I never shall! When I die I shall leave nothing to build hospitals or found churches, nothing for the indigent poor, nothing for anybody who hasn't the right to it."

He was a shrewd man, in many ways brilliant. He had one of those extraordinarily nimble minds which are the peculiar possession of the accountant and the bookmaker. There was no need for him to take any extra precautions. He had sized up Hex and knew that he had a foe worthy of his steel, but felt quite competent to meet all the machinations which the most ingenious and most unscrupulous philanthropist could devise.

If he scrutinised a little more closely the documents which came before him in the ordinary course of business for his signature, if he watched with a little more care the companions of his son, if he was a little more suspicious of all the business proposals which came before him from outside sources, and read into them some sinister scheme of Captain Hex to secure his subscription, it was not an unusual care for an unprecedented suspicion, nor a particularly remarkable scrutiny which he exercised, for he was by nature careful.

Of Hex he saw nothing for the first three days. A private detective whom he had employed to shadow the philanthropist reported that he spent most of his time in the private sitting-room of his hotel with his companion, the tall, solemn soldier with whom he occasionally went abroad.

He met Hex in the street by accident on the fourth day and crossed the road to greet him.

"Well," demanded Mr. Match boisterously, his eyes agleam, "how goes the robbery under arms—the great-turf fraud—the Jim the Penman-Ship?"

Hex laughed.

"Fine," he said. "I reckon your money is as good as in my pocket."

Match roared his merriment.

"Have you found a scheme?"

Hex shook his head.

"Not really—but I'm picking it up little by little. Watts invented the steam engine through seeing a kettle boil. I'm watching the extraordinary effect of large self-confidence upon the security of wealth."

"Watch!" said the other, and put out his hand. "You're going to get eye-strain."

He was going on, but Hex laid his hand on his arm.

"Wait—there's one thing I want to tell you," he said. "There are a dozen ways I could get the money from you, but they're all dishonest. I could forge your name as easily as anything—I should have made a most successful criminal—I could burgle your stately mansion at Morpeth—I've reconnoitred the ground and it's dead easy to get through the window above the portico—"

"Try it," said the other significantly.

"Oh, I know all about the burglar alarms, but I could make them inoperative with a gimlet and a wire in a matter of moments. I could impersonate you so that your own son would be deceived. But none of these things appeal to me. There isn't any art in them—I should just hate to take the money. But you're a difficult proposition. You're too big —there's nothing really mean about you."

"Flatterer," smiled Mr. Match.

"It's a fact. I could never get you to buy a share in buried treasure, or bluff you into believing that I know all about your past life. You're just an honest rascal making a fortune out of people's necessity and so far as I can see you have only one weak spot."

Mr. Match looked at him quizzically.

"Let me know that and I am fortified," he said.

"You are too confident of yourself," said Hex. "That's where your undoing lies."

"Prove it."

"I can prove it all right," said Hex.

They were near his hotel and the hour was one.

"Come and lunch with me, if I promise you that I will neither dope, sandbag nor hypnotise you."

"Done!" said Mr. Match heartily. "We will discuss this matter further —you amuse me."

It was not until the lunch was over that Mr. Match again approached the subject. Throughout the meal Hex kept up a light, continuous flow of amusing reminiscence and Mr. Match found him an agreeable companion.

"You were talking about my self-confidence and how it might ruin me. I am interested. Please elucidate."

Hex shrugged his shoulders.

"What I mean is that you have confidence in the processes of business and in your own ability to handle any situation which has to do with the transference of money. For example, if I asked you for a cheque for £8,000 at this moment and you gave me that cheque, you would be quite satisfied in your mind that you would be able to prevent that money from going to charity."

The shipper thought for a moment.

"Yes," he said. "I think I can say with confidence—it may be over-confidence but I don't think it is—that I could give you —in fact, I am quite willing to give you at this moment—a crossed cheque for £8,000."

"You think that you could stop it."

The other nodded.

"You would probably post-date it till tomorrow."

Match nodded again.

"And such is your confidence in the etiquette and practice of banking that you would not be one penny the worse off."

"Exactly," said the other, "though it might put you in rather a hole, my friend."

"Whether it would or not," said Hex, offering his cigarette case, "I challenge you to do so, and I promise you that if I do not get the value of that cheque applied to the purpose I design it, I will not bother you again."

For a moment the shipping man looked at him and then, with a little grin and with that quickness which characterised all his movements, he slipped a chequebook from one pocket and a fountain pen from another, and wrote. Hex, looking across the table, saw that the cheque was dated for the following day. He noted that under the amount Mr. Match wrote:

"This cheque must only be passed on the personal authorisation of the payer."

He signed it with a flourish, crossed it with two heavy strokes and handed it to his companion with a smile. Hex drew a long sigh of relief.

"Thank you," he said. "I see you have made it payable to bearer."

"The bearer will have some difficulty in getting it," said Mr. Match.

Mr. Match drove straight back to his office and without a moment's delay called up his bank on the telephone.

"That you, Gilbert? It's Theodore Match speaking. I have just given a cheque for £8,000, payable to bearer—got that? The number of the cheque is A.B. 714312—got that? I stop payment of that cheque and it is not to be cashed or debited to my account under any circumstances. I will give you confirmation in writing."

It may be said of Theodore Match that his pleasures were mainly intellectual. He had found his principal joy in life in pitting his wits against wits as shrewd or nearly as shrewd as his own, and it is true that he accounted success less by the money that that success brought to him than by the satisfaction of having outwitted his opponent. Whether or not Hex knew his man before he came to Newcastle, it is certain that he understood him now.

Match did not regard the money as of any great consequence. He took a keen pleasure in the game for the game's sake and it was in this spirit of eager interest that he awaited the culmination of his enemy's plan.

His watcher brought him two items of news that afternoon, one that the soldier-companion of Captain Hex had gone to London by the first train, the second that Hex had hired the window of a small confectioner's shop in the main street for two days, and that the contents of that window were being hurriedly removed to make way for an interesting exhibit. No other happening marked that afternoon. Having secured his window, Hex did not fill it. It was not until the following afternoon that he showed his hand, simultaneously with the issue of the evening papers.

At half past two Mr. Match received a telegram from London.

HEARTIEST CONGRATULATIONS AND THANKS FOR YOUR HELP.

It was signed "Smith."

"Now who the dickens is Smith?" asked Match with a frown.

He was cogitating when Tom, his young hopeful, burst into the room.

"I say, Governor," he gasped, "you didn't tell me you were going to do it!"

"Do what?" asked Mr. Match, suspiciously.

"Why," said the young hopeful, "that Prince's Fund; you told me you would not contribute a cent!"

Mr. Match was on his feet.

"And how much have I contributed?" he asked quietly.

"£8,000. It's in the evening papers. That fellow Hex has got a window in High Street pasted round with appeals for the Prince's Fund, and a photographic enlargement of your cheque in the centre."

Mr. Match collapsed into his chair. "Good lor'!" he said. "What do the papers say?"

The young man took a paper and read:

"We understand that the Prince's Fund for Merchant Seamen is the richer by £8,000 through the generosity of Mr. Theodore Match of this city, a cheque for this amount having been given by our patriotic fellow-citizen."

"Good lor'!" said Match again. "So that was his dodge! He couldn't get it for himself, and so he got it for the fund."

"Did you give him a cheque?"

Mr. Match nodded.

"But I stopped it," he said. "That fellow's too clever for me."

"But you aren't going to let it go through?" said his agitated hopeful.

"Don't be a fool, Tom," said Mr. Match calmly. "Stopping a cheque for one of Hex's infernal schemes and stopping a cheque for a big national fund are two different matters. He's got me all right. Don't you see what would happen if I repudiated my gift? I should be pilloried from one end of the country to the other."

With a deep sigh he reached for the telephone and gave the number.

"That you, Gilbert? With reference to that cheque I stopped yesterday—yes, the one for £8,000. It is now in order. Let it go through."

He pressed a bell, summoned his secretary, and dictated a confirmation. He went home that night a silent, thoughtful man, and answered the congratulations of the few privileged friends who could approach him on the subject somewhat absently.

The next morning when he got to his office, he found his banker waiting for him.

"That cheque was cleared very quickly," said Gilbert.

"Cleared?" said Mr. Match in surprise.

The other nodded.

"It was cleared soon after I got your message yesterday afternoon, through the London and Midland Bank of Newcastle. By the way, I see that there is a contradiction about your gift in this morning's paper."

Mr. Match took the paper in his hand without a word and read—.

We find we were in error in describing the charity which benefited by Mr. Match's munificence as the Prince's Fund. This error was due to the fact that a facsimile of the cheque was shown in the High Street amidst a number of appeals to support the Prince's charity. The money has been devoted to Captain Hex's Cottage Homes for Seamen's Families.

Mr. Match put down the paper.

"I gave the cheque," he said, talking aloud to himself. "I stopped the cheque and then I authorised its payment, just as he said I would. It was clever. He took the cheque, paid it into the London and Midland—he must have opened a special account in Newcastle for some such purpose—and started the story about my having subscribed to the Prince's Fund knowing that the first thing I would do would be to cancel the stoppage of the cheque—clever! Yes, I was overconfident, all right!"

He picked up the telephone.

"Give me the Station Hotel." Then after a pause: "Is Captain Hex there? Put him through, please. Is that you, Hex?

"Yes," said the cheerful voice of Hex.

"When you get tired of your career of crime," said Mr. Match, "I can give you a partnership in this firm."

"Not on your life," said Hex. "You're not going to get your money back that way!"

When Mr. Match put down the telephone he was laughing softly to himself.

CHAPTER III

THE FOILING OF MR. HARRY B. KINGBERRY

When Captain Hex marked down a reluctant and generally unconscious subscriber to any of those naval and military charities in which he interested himself, it was his invariable practice to make a study of his victim.

The reputation of Mr. Harry B. Kingberry was such as to attract such a connoisseur of unearned Wealth as Captain Hex, and since Mr. Kingberry was one of those shy individuals who conducted their business from a very small office on the third floor of a very big business block, and made visits to London no more than twice a week, and those only for the briefest duration, Captain Hex had no opportunities for studying his subject in town, and must needs reconnoitre the wild country in which he lived.

At seven o'clock one autumn evening Captain Hex arrived at the little market town of Budleigh Milton, in the county of Berkshire. It was a small railway station, lit dimly, and he found himself and his companion, ex-Private Belshazzar Smith, two of half-a-dozen passengers who had alighted at this unpromising destination. Of these, two particularly attracted the attention of Captain Hex, who was very naturally observant and suspicious.

"I wonder who they are?" asked Hex curiously.

Drawn up by the kerb was a large motor-car. A footman was waiting, and after a brief exchange of words the two men got into the car, which was driven off.

"Whose machine is that?" asked Hex of a waiting cabman.

"That's Mr. Kingsberry's, sir. They are going up to the 'All."

"Mr. Kingsberry's, eh?" mused Hex. "Who are the visitors?" he demanded shamelessly.

The cabman was very informative, as apparently also had been the chauffeur. The two gentlemen had come from London on business, and they were going back on the ten o'clock train.

He engaged the cabman to drive him to the Red Lion, the one hotel in the town, and over a dinner of cold beef and pickles he discussed with Belshazzar Smith his plans for the morrow.

"He's a pretty tough case, Belshazzar Smith," said Hex, sipping his coffee thoughtfully. "I cannot see our technical school for disabled Tommie being started on Harry's good money."

He looked at his watch.

"I am going to the station at 9.30, and I want you to be there somewhere in the background. I don't know exactly what is going to happen, but I have a notion that were are going to get next to a lot of excitement."

It was a quarter to ten when the staring headlamps of Mr. Kingsberry's big limousine swung into the station yard. The car pulled up just short of the entrance, and two men alighted. So far as Hex could see they were the same two whose departure he had witnessed with such curiosity. They did not pass through the booking-hall, but after a glance at his watch, one of them turned and said—

"We have fifteen minutes to wait. We had better stay out here."

They strolled to the far end of the pavement before the station premises and leant against the wooden rails which separated the station yard from the deserted platform.

Hex passed through the booking-hall, walked quickly and noiselessly along the platform, stopping in the shelter of the last of the station buildings. From where he stood he could hear their voices speaking in low tones. He edged a little closer, and, peering through the darkness, saw their backs turned to him. The only cover available was that afforded by a large sheet-iron advertisement which had been nailed to the palings, and, crouching, he moved stealthily to this shelter. If they looked over the railings and downward they could not avoid seeing him.

Their voices were still too low to offer any clue to their conversation. He heard the words "old man" and caught the word "beans," and heard one of them laugh softly. Then ensued a mumbled conversation which was wholly unintelligible. Presently he heard another word which sounded like "Van Witt." Then of a sudden the voice of one rose in consternation.

"I've left the paper behind," he said, and cursed.

"What paper?" asked the other.

"The drawing. I put it down on the seat in the billiard-room."

Another mumble. They were discussing the advisability of returning, the the second voice opposed such a course.

"I can remember it, It is very simple."

"But suppose the servants—"

"They won't know what it means."

Footsteps resounded on the platform, a distant whistle of the train brought the men towards the booking-hall, and Hex, rising from his uncomfortable position, went back the way he had come. He met them face to face as they emerged on the platform, but he could distinguish nothing which would ever enable him to identify them. He noted, however, that neither of the men wore gloves, and that one of them had some sort of design tattooed on the back of his hand. He found Belshazzar Smith pacing up and down the station yard.

"Belshazzar Smith," he said quickly, "have you got your return ticket to London?"

"I have, sir."

"Go back by this train. Get in the same compartment as these two men, and find out where one of them lives. They are probably going to separate in London. You must track the one that is easiest. On second thoughts, you had better not get into the same compartment. They may spot you following them."

Hex waited until the train had gone out, then made his way back to his hotel, unpacked his electric torch, and set forth to tramp the four miles which separated the town of Budleigh Milton from the residential estate of Mr. Kingberry.

The billiard-room was an apartment modernly panneled in rosewood, wonderfully roofed in Moorish plasterwork, and possessed mullioned windows in the style of the 15th century. The billiard-table was an expensive and impressive piece of furniture with legs carved in the Queen Anne style. The raised settees were of Sheraton design, and the rich-looking cabinet in the corner was a magnificent example of the gramophone period.

"Holy smoke," murmured Captain Hex, "the fellow who furnished this room was an artist."

He was evidently searching for something of importance, for after his curious and general survey of the apartment he began a systematic search of the room. It was on one of the morocco-leather settees that he discovered what he had been looking for. It was a half-sheet of notepaper folded into small compass. By the light of his electric torch he examined the paper. It contained no more than a pencil-drawing of a circle with a palm-tree in the centre. The palm-tree was not well-drawn, but even the veriest tyro who knows little about art can draw a palm-tree.

Captain Hex took a pencil from his pocket and rapidly transferred the design to his shirt-cuff, replaced the paper where he had found it, and turned to go.

He had taken two stealthy strides toward the open window through which he had entered, when there was a soft click and the billiard-table was flooded with light from the shaded lamps above.

In the doorway stood a man.

In the subdued light Hex saw that he was wearing a dressing-gown of execrable design. He was a stout man, and bald, except for a fringe of hair above his ears, and that he was agitated Captain Hex gathered from the fact that the revolver he held in his hand wobbled indecisively. Hex took his cigarette-holder from his lips and nodded courteously.

"Good morning," he said pleasantly. "I hope I haven't disturbed you."

The man im the doorway spluttered.

"By—by gad, sir!" he said, with difficulty disguising a trembling of the lips. "What the devil—smoking, by gad!"

"Sorry," said Hex, throwing away the cigarette. "I thought you wouldn't mind my smoking in your billiard-room."

"What are you doing here? Who are you? Burglary, eh?" roared the man in the dressing-gown (a green crane on a purple ground swallowing a pink fish). Hex noted the design and shuddered.

"Not a burglar, sir; if you will sit down I will explain," he said easily.

"Sit down! By thunder! Here! Jones! Jackson! Jevons!" he shouted back into the darkness, and there was a rustle of stockinged feet.

"You can save yourself the trouble," said Hex calmly. "I am, in a sense, the police."

"Eh?"

The other stared at him suspiciously, uneasily.

"My card," said Hex, waving off the two irresolute servants.

He handed the white oblong with a flourish.

"'Captain Hex, D.S.O.'," read Mr. Kingberry. "'Hex's Detective Agency. Restitution Department.'"

Put Down for £4,000

He looked up at his prisoner.

"That's my name," said Hex, "and now you will understand why I called—I see you've had visitors."

He pointed to a table on which stood three glasses and a soda-water syphon.

"Eh?" said Mr. Kingberry more easily. "What's that to do with you?"

Hex shrugged his shoulders and sank gracefully into the depths of large club-chair.

"Let us dispense with unnecessary witnesses," he said with a significant nod.

The man in the dressing-gown (Hex blinked at it, fascinated) jerked his head to the two men.

"Wait in the hall. I'll call you when I want you," he growled, but carefully closed the door behind him.

"Now look here, Captain," he began mildly, but Hex stopped him with a gesture.

"Let us come down to brass tacks," he said, "and settle a matter which is greatly distressing me. Sit down, Mr. Raspberry."

"Kingberry!" snarled the man. "By gad—"

"Cut all that retired colonel stuff," said Hex, "and listen.

With the greatest reluctance the bald man obeyed, mumbling menacing noises.

"I am the head of two or three philanthropic enterprises," said Hex. "They are designed for the benefit of the discharged soldier, his wife and his family. I secure my funds by bleeding profiteers, food-sharks and money-hogs who have made fat out of this blessed war. It is my practice to force 'em to pay against their wills. I have put you down for £4,000."

"You want to kid me that you broke into my house in the middle of the night to ask for a subscription. It won't do."

Mr. Kingberry got up.

"You can explain that to the police," he said, reaching for the bell-push in the panneled wall, "and as for subscribing—bah!"

"Bah yourself!" said Hex. "Don't ring—I haven't finished yet. I say that I had marked you down. In fact, I had almost decided that you should be my next contributor, but—"

He shook his head sadly.

"Mr. Kingberry," he said, "I am willing to take any money but crooked money."

There was a dead silence.

"What do you mean?" asked Kingberry, clearing his throat, but husky nevertheless.

Hex looked at the table with the three glasses.

"You've had visitors," he said softly.

Mr. Kingberry jumped to his feet.

"And what if I have?" he demanded in a strident voice. "What's that to do with you? Can't a gentleman have—"

He stopped, for Hex had suddenly taken his eyes away from Mr. Kingberry'a face and was gazing intently at the table where the glasses stood.

"Hello!" he said.

He walked to the table and picked up half-a-dozen small objects which had escaped his notice and now, as his eyes became accustomed to the semi-gloom of all that part of the room which was not illuminated by the table-lamps, he could see more clearly.

"What have you got there?" asked Mr.Kingberry, starting up.

Hex held his open palm under the lamp and examined its contents.

"Beans," he said, "horse-beans, beans!"

Suddenly he remembered a word he had heard one of the men use. In his hand were six familiar kidney-shaped objects; to be exact, there were six and a half, for one had evidently been broken in two.

No further examination was possible, because Mr. Kingberry, with a quick movement, jerked the contents from the intruder's hand. Hex looked at the man in surprise. His face had gone dirty-white. His hand was trembling. and emotion so overpowered him that for some time he could not speak. When he did he pointed to the open window.

"That's the way you came and that's the way you'd better go," he said shakily. "I give you a chance that you will never get again—get out!"

"Good morning," said Hex, and leapt lightly through the window to the garden-bed below.

Belshazzar Smith had a brief and uninteresting story to tell. He had followed one of the men home to Walthamstow. The man's name was Diver, and, so far as could be discovered by Belshazzar Smith—it was fortunate that Diver was known to the owner of a coffee-stall at the corner of the street—he worked at the North India Docks in some capacity. He wore a uniform with brass buttons, but what his duties were the coffee-stall keeper was unable to say. He thought they were something important, because Diver lived in a good house and frequently came home from his work in a taxicab

"That's good enough," said Hex, jumping out of bed. "Get me my shaving-water, Belshazzar. We are going back to town on the next train."

"Ain't we going to see Kingberry?" asked the astonished Belshazzar.

"Not to-day," replied Captain Hex grimly.

That day he spent pursuing inquiries in the City among Kingberry's business acquaintances. It was a fact that nobody quite knew how the millionaire, who was probably not a millionaire at all but an extremely rich man nonetheless, had made his money. Yes, he did a big trade, principally with Sweden and Holland, and with the Dutch colonies and Spain.

A merchant in Mincing Lane gave some further information. Kingberry had a licence to export fodder and cattle-food of various kinds.

"He has often bought horse-beans from me," said the factor. "In fact, he does a pretty big trade in this line. Some he buys here, some he imports from Spain. As a matter of fact, I happen to know that he is shipping a cargo to Holland this week—I sold him twenty tons myself."

"Can you tell me by what ship these beans are going?" asked Hex, interested.

The merchant rang the bell.

"I can give you that information, I think," he replied, and when his clerk came in he asked: "Where did we deliver those horse-beans for Kingberry?!

"To the North India Docks, sir," said the clerk.

"How were they marked?" asked the merchant.

"I will tell you in a minute, sir."

The clerk disappeared, and presently came back.

"They are being shipped by the Jan Van Witt," he said.

A light dawned upon him.

"Thank you very much," he said.

On the morning that followed Captain Hex, armed with a letter of introduction from a very important Government Department, called upon the Superintendent of the North India Docks, and found that genial man communicative.

"I see," said the Superintendent, with a glance at the letter, "you want permission to go anywhere in the docks. There's no difficulty about that. I don't suppose you are going to try to smuggle contraband aboard."

"Hardly," said Hex.

He turned suddenly so that his back was to the doorway, and heard a cheery voice hail the Superintendent through the open door.

"That was Mr. Kingberry. You have heard of him? He was a war shipper. One of the biggest of 'em," said the Superintendent.

"I have heard of him," said Hex.

"He is sending a big cargo off the Rotterdam, and he usually comes down and watches the loading and examination."

"Tell me this," asked Hex: "What is the procedure when boats go from here to Rotterdam? Are they liable to search on the North Sea?"

The Superintendent nodded.

"All ships are liable to search in war time," he said, "but as a matter of fact, when a ship clears with a cargo from London or from any of the coast ports and doesn't touch a foreign port it is seldom examined. We make the inspection of the cargo here and give the ship a certificate of innocence."

"But isn't that dangerous?" asked Hex.

The Superintendent shook his head with a smile.

"We have a special staff who do nothing but break cargo and examine it," he said. "In a shipment like this, for example, which Mr. Kingberry is sending over, we probably open fifty barrels haphazard, and turn them out to see if anything was concealed. If there was the slightest suspicion, every barrel would be opened.

"What is it you look for mostly?" asked Hex.

"Rubber," said the Superintendent. "That's the stuff they are trying to get by hook or crook. A man who could send a ton of rubber into Germany would make a small fortune. The profit is nearly a thousand per cent. She has been getting it in some way or another, and there has been a lot of trouble about the leakage, so naturally we keep a bright look-out. The Dutch do all they can to discourage the traffic, and the steamship line which does most of the carrying between here and Holland offers big rewards for the detection of contraband. Naturally, they stand to lose very heavily if the contraband cargo is found aboard."

Hex made his way along the docks, but before he reached the berth where the Jan Van Witt lay he was joined by the Superintendent.

"I thought I'd walk along with you," said the official. "Here you see the work I was telling you about."

The dock was covered with barrels, up-ended, standing in rows, and two officials in uniform, accompanied by workmen, had just at that moment opened one of the barrels, and the workmen were turning its contents on a sheet of sacking.

"Beans,"said the Superintendent.

Hex watched. When the inspection was completed the beans were returned to the barrel, the lid was securely fastened, and the officials resumed their stroll, stopping before another barrel, which was opened and treated in exactly the same way.

"They will probably examine twenty or thirty," said the Superintendent.

"Will you tell me the names of those two officials?" asked Hex quietly.

"The first is a man named Benson. The second is a man named Diver. They have taken the place of two men who have been dismissed for irregularity."

Hex nodded. He observed Mr. Kingberry hovering in the background, smoking a large cigar, and keeping an eye on the inspection of his cargo.

"May I look at those barrels?"

"Why, surely," said the Superintendent.

Hex walked to the first and examined it, but did not see what he sought. At the fifth barrel, however, he stopped. On the barrel-head, stencilled in dull red, almost indistinguishable since the other markings were of the same colour, was a small circle, inside of which there was a small palm-tree.

Neither the sixth nor the seventh nor the eighth barrel, but the eleventh and twelfth carried the sign.

"I wonder if you would do me a favour?"

"What is that," asked the dock official.

"I should like to have this barrel opened."

The Superintendent hesitated.

"There is no reason why you shouldn't," he said after a pause, and called Diver.

The man turned back, and it was at that moment that Kingberry recognised his midnight visitor. He dropped his cigar and walked quickly in the direction of the group.

"What's up?" he asked.

He did not look at Hex, but Hex looked at him. The same grey look was on his face that he had seen that night in the billiard-room.

"This gentleman wants to see this barrel broached," said the Superintendent. "Open it, will you, Diver."

"I have inspected this one, sir."

"Not his one," volunteered a workman.

"Open it," said the Superintendent.

"Why open it again?" protested Kingberry violently. "I suppose the fellow has been telling you yarns. He is a burglar, that's what he is. He broke into my house the other night."

Superintedent Fraser turned a pair of cold eyes on the millionaire.

"That may or may not be so, sir, "but I can see no objection to the cask being broached. Open it, one of you men."

The workmen prized off the top and poured the contents upon the sacking.

Hex gasped, for there were only beans. He looked into the barrel, tapped it and examined the bottom of the barrel without result other than discovering that it was made of wood.

"Are you satisfied?" asked Mr. Kingberry.

"No," said Hex. "I will see another barrel emptied."

He pointed to another that bore the sign of the circle and the palm-tree. Again the top was removed. Again the contents streamed out onto the sacking. Beans and nothing else!

"Put them back," said the Superintendent.

They were scoped back into the barrel, except one which rolled from the sacking next to Hex's feet. He stooped and picked it up with the intention of replacing it. It was an unconscious act, for it mattered little if the barrel were short of one bean or twenty. He tossed it into the barrel but undershot his mark. The bean fell and the bean bounced.

He darted upon it, lifted it up, and tried to break it. It bent but it did not break, and when the pressure of his finger was released it straightened out agsin, just as any well-conducted piece of india-rubber, moulded and painted, would do.

In the subsequent search twenty-four barrels of rubber were discovered. The fact that they were all shaped like horse-beans did not make them any the less rubber. The dock police arrested Mr. Kingberry and his two associates, and Hex went back to the Superintendent's office.

"It was clear to me," he explained, "that Kingberry wanted to pass something through the docks without inspection. He evidently got into touch with the two inspectors and paid them well. How well, we shall discover. In order that they should not examine those containing the rubber, he had those barrels specially marked with the circle and the palm-tree, and your examiners tactfully overlooked them.

"I really went down to get a donation to a charitable fund, and I certainly had no intention of being a clever Alec of the Intelligence Department. I have lost a possible subscriber."

"Don't forget the reward of the shipping company," said the Superintendent.

Indeed Captain Hex did not forget. For a week he practically sat on their step, haunted their ante-rooms, button-holed their directors, and finally left with the nucleus of that fund which eventually produced his technical school.

"Which shows, Belshazzar Smith," said Captain Hex to his lieutenant, "that it possible to get money quite honestly."

"As 'Errick say," said Belshazzar Smith, "'it has been.'"

"Don't let "Errick say 'has been,' said Captain Hex. "Let him say 'horse-bean.'"

CHAPTER IV

MR. MONTAGUE SLUIS IS CAUGHT NAPPING—

There was a sound of revelry by night in the gilded halls of the Grand Revendriex Restaurant. The hour was late, but the revelry was very exclusive, being confined to the guests of Mr. Montague Sluis.

There was a coon band in attendance; there was a wonderful buffet piled high with uncouponed viands and forbidden ices, and champagne in unlimited quantities. Cups amber and cups crimson glittered refreshingly; peaches, grapes, early strawberries—all that was rare and refreshing from orchard and hothouse—were displayed invitingly In the silver épergnes at the back of the sideboard.

Well might Mr. Sluis spend his money with seeming recklessness. He was a director of fourteen companies, and until this horrible war had brought sorrow and penury into business circles he had been a director of ten others, the names of which ended in "Gesellschaft".

Mr. Sluis was as true a Briton as ever was born in Mannheim and naturalised in Whitehall. He had subscribed heavily to war bonds. He had denounced Germany in terms which the Kaiser could scarcely have read without a shudder. He handed over all his shares and holdings in enemy concerns to his brother in Holland. He had heroically foregone the dividends accruing to him from his association with the various "Gesellschaften," and had allowed them to accumulate in Amsterdam, and as often as twice a week his beautiful steam launch carried parties of wounded soldiers to view the natural beauties of river scenery, in a large portion of which Mr. Sluis was financially interested

The feast of music and movement was at its height when the skeleton appeared in the doorway. He was a good-looking skeleton—in correct evening dress, wearing on the lapel of his coat a silver badge which it is the honourable privilege of a discharged soldier or officer to wear, and he walked with a slight limp. He nodded easily to the janitor, who took it for granted that he was an invited guest, and after a cursory examination of the room he strolled across to the little but expensive knot of stout gentlemen who stood in one corner of the room surveying the revels with an approving eye.

Mr. Sluis, who was a stocky man, with a mop of curly blond hair and a disposition to perspire at the slightest excuse, fixed the newcomer through his pince-nez and frowned.

Mr. Sluis Is Unmoved

"I thought I'd look you up," said Captain Hex cheerily.

"Didn't I invite you?" asked Mr. Sluis meaningly and without any warmth or enthusiasm in his voice.

"To be exact, you didn't," said Hex; "but I thought that on this festive occasion, when the hearts of the hardest are necessarily softened at the sight of so much beauty, you might take a more favourable view of my proposition."

"Captain Hex," said Mr. Sluis, closing his eyes—a gesture of dignity which was habitual in him—and raising a large, stout hand, "I haf giffen moneys in colossal sums to charity. To-day, yesterday, it seems for eternity, you haf pestered me with requests that I should subscribe heaffily—I repeat heaffily."

"I heard you." said Hex—"heaffily, you said."

"To your Cottage Homes for Soldiers—a society which is not efen in the list of permissible charities to collect for."

"Quite right," said Hex.

"And now you come to me, mit all my friendts here, uninfited, and, if you will pardon me, objectionable."

"Don't say that," pleaded Hex.

"Objectionable, I repeat," said Mr. Sluis. "Why? To give you £5,000. It is absurd."

"I don't agree with you," said Hex. "You see, Mr. Sluis, I have to get money. My hobbies are expensive. I have made a hobby of helping the discharged soldier, who is, as a rule, a most unpicturesque individual out of uniform, and does not appeal to the charitably-minded. Consequently, my task is a difficult one. Dowager Duchesses do not object to driving in the most exclusive thoroughfares of London with men in hospital blue; indeed they feel honoured by this exercise. Put the man of hospital blue into a reach-me-down suit, a blue collar, and a green tie, and put a bowler hat on his head in place of his uniform cap, and he passes from the hero class—"

"I tell you definite," said Mr. Sluis, " I gif you nothing."

"Then I am afraid I shall have to take from you the sum of £5,000."

Mr. Sluis smiled. You might have thought that the idea of anybody taking £5,000 from him amused him. As a matter of fact, the mere prospect would have given him exquisite pain, but because he did not believe that there was in the world a power which could extract this enormous sum from his banking account he permitted himself to advertise his amusement.

"There is nothing else?" he asked sarcastically.

"Yes," said Hex, "I'll have a drink."

He made his way to the buffet, selected his drink with great care, helped himself to a cigar, and with a little nod to the small and speechless group, faded from the room.

Captain Hex drove straight away to the House of Commons, at which grave institution he had dined. He knew the House was sitting all night, and that his one friend amongst all the legislators would be expecting him. Septimus O'Bryan who, I hasten to add, was not related to any other O'Bryan, had recently made the acquaintance of the philanthropic Captain Hex. They had met in exceptional circumstances, and indeed O'Bryan was an exceptional man. On the outbreak of war he had disappeared from view for the greater part of two years. It was rumoured that he had gone to Australia and to America, but in truth he had enlisted in an English regiment, under a false name, had been wounded and discharged, and his identity might have gone unguessed but for Hex meeting him unexpectedly and recognising in this member of Parliament a man who had fought in his own company.

There are many who will not believe this story, and very few people in the House of Commons who have any inkling of it. But there was one man who knew, and that man was Captain Hex, D.S.O., who had recommended "Private Briery" for the Military Medal, which Septimus O'Bryan, M.P., cherished amongst his secret treasures.

"Did ye find him?" he asked as he came across the lobby to meet Hex.

"I found him."

"Did he put up the money?"

"He did not," said Hex.

"Bad luck to him," said the legislator. "Come and have a drink and tell me what you want to see me about. It's an all-night sitting, and we shan't be disturbed."

Over their refreshment Hex explained the position.

"Of course, everybody knows Sluis is a Boche; that doesn't help any," he said. "I'll tell you what I want you to do. You are acquainted with Sluis. Frankly, that is why I sought you out yesterday and put the matter before you."

"But he's no friend of mine," said Septimus quickly.

"I know that, Septimus." said Hex nodding, "but you can tell me something about him. What is his weakness?"

"Faith, he has no weakness except a love of money," said Septimus.

"Has he any hobby?"

"Getting more money, the black-hearted hound," said the member, "and, be-hivens! I nearly forgot his pearls."

"Pearls?"

The other nodded vehemently.

"'Tis the foinest collection in the world he has. Have ye never heard of them?"

"Pearls, eh?"

"Ropes of them; stacks of them. 'Tis his passion."

"That is good news," said Hex thoughtfully.

Shadowed

The following days Hex pursued his inquries, aided by the faithful Belshazzar Smith, who succeeded in getting into touch with one of Mr Sluis' body servants.

"Met him in a public-house off Grosvenor Square," said Belshazzar, "in the saloon bar an' quite the gentleman. As Keats says, 'Conviviality!'"

"What's the matter with 'Errick?" asked Hex; "isn't he on duty to-day?"

"Well, sir, 'Errick made a similar remark about wine; he said—"

"Tell us about the gentlemanly footman."

"Well, sir, I asked him as per your instructions, about the pearls. They're kept in a strong-room on the first floor—opening from the library. There's always a man on duty day and night."

"You asked that, did you?"

"Yes, sir—you told me to. Also I asked whether Mr. Sluis buys pearls privately or only through jewellers."

"That's good," said Hex admiringly. "Really, Belshazzar, you seem to have succeeded most admirably."

"Tact," said Belshazzar Smith proudly, "is one of the things I pride myself on."

"And with reason," said Hex. "I wonder you weren't pinched."

He had not finished speaking when there came a knock at the door. Belshazzar Smith opened it to discover a district messenger with a letter written on House of Commons stationery, addressed to Captain Hex, and marked "Urgent."

It was from Mr. Septimus O'Bryan, and ran:—

"Dear Captain,—I was in the city this morning, and I heard all about you. It appears that your practice of extracting money from the loathsome millionaire has earnt you indecent fame. Sluis is on your track. Both you and your man are being watched by private detectives. I thought you ought to know this. Sluis is an unforgiving devil, and has made up his mind to have you."

Hex folded the letter.

"I had noticed the detectives," he said; "so had you, Belshazzarr Smith."

"Me!" said the startled Belshazzar. "No, sir, I didn't notice anything."

Captain Hex laughed softly.

"I was watching you from the window. I saw them following you in the street and shepherd you into the house. Come here." He led the way to the window. "Do you see that man at the corner picking his teeth? That's one of them. Where's the other? Oh, there he is."

He indicated at the further end of the street a quietly-dressed man who was standing on the edge of the kerb, apparently reading an evening newspaper.

Belshazzar Smith looked serious.

"Does this mean we are going to get into trouble?" he asked.

"I should worry," said Captain Hex.

It was not a pleasant task which Mr. Sluis had set his sleuthhounds. Captain Hex was a very nimble and energetic person. It seemed to the weary man who dogged his footsteps that he would never tire. The annoying thing was that he insisted upon walking. To follow a man in a taxicab when unlimited expenses are allowed is a luxurious proceeding. Even to follow him on a bus has its merits, but to walk and walk and walk from ten in the morning to five in the afternoon brought iron to the soul of two amiable members of the detective agency which had been engaged by Mr Sluis.

But their patience was rewarded. On the fourth day of their vigil Captain Hex made a visit to Hatton Gardens, and there purchased from a dealer in such things a very handsome jewel-case, on which he had engraved his initials, "R. H." This he carried home with him. The case, as one of the detectives learnt, was empty, the firm in question being a manufacturer and supplying most of the wholesale jewellers in the neighbourhood.

The day following produced no results to the watchers, who had reported their discoveries to their employer. The next day, however, was one rich in possibilities. Captain Hex drove to Willington Arcade in Piccadilly, at the end of which stands the dazzling establishment of the Persian Diamond Company. You cannot pass its windows on a sunny day without smoked glasses for from a score of beds of velvet and rich silk flash and scintillate, gleam and glow, gorgeous brilliants and milk-white pearls, most of which can be purchased under 15s.

To this maker of artificial stones went Hex, and his purchases were large. He bought pearls, a whole string of them, of moderate size and of perfect colour, and he showed an almost fastidious taste in their selection.

"They look almost like real, don't they," said the smiling shopman, and it was at this moment that the detective strolled in aimlessly and began to examine one of the show cases.

"None but a connoisseur would tell the difference," said Hex. "Will you string them together for me?"

He waited till this was completed, watched the "pearls" being placed in an ornamental case, paid £6, their price, and with his purchase under his arm stepped out in the arcade.

Mr. Sluis Sets a Trap

That night there was a conference in the library of Mr Sluis. He gathered his friends round him to tell them the good news.

"You would nefer think it possible—such audacity!" he beamed. "I haf had a telephone message from Hex offering to sell me his pearls."

He laughed long and loud.

"What have you done?" demanded one of his cronies.

"I haf infited him here to-night to negotiate," he chuckled again and slapped his stout knee, then he lugged a watch from his pocket. "In fife minutes the little mouse will walk into the lions' den," he said jovially.

The "little mouse" came in later, very cheery, apparently unresentful at the cavalier treatment he had received. He carried under his arm the jewel case of blue leather which had cost him much more than his pearl purchases of that morning. Mr. Sluis was all affability, and with his own moist hands brought forward a chair.

"You want to sell pearls, eh?" he smiled. "Well, well, I can purchase pearls. I haf the finest collection in Europe."

"So I have heard," said Captain Hex, "and I am anxious that you should add these to your collection."

He opened the case arid displayed a string of beautiful white shimmering objects. Mr. Sluis made a pretence of examining them.

"Very beautiful," he said. "What are you asking for these?"

"£6,000," said Ilex.

Mr. Sluis shrugged his shoulders and gave a sidelong glance at his companions.

"It is a lot of money," he said. "A string of that description should not be worth much more than £2,000, but I am not a haggler, and I daresay if you come to-morrow night about this time we can make a deal."

"At the price?" asked Hex anxiously.

Mr. Sluis smiled.

"Certainly. I would like to do you a turn and I will not haggle mit you."

Captain Hex drew a deep sigh of relief.

"There is only one thing," he said softly. "I should like you to pay me—"

"In cash, of course," said Mr. Sluis, "you don't like cheques. But perhaps you will tell me how you came into possession of these pearls?"

"I bought them for a purpose," said Hex, "and now I am anxious to sell them. That is the only explanation I care to offer."

"Surely, surely," said Mr. Sluis quickly. "I should not pry into your business, eh? Very good, Captain Hex."

He offered his hand.

"Till to-morrow night at six o'clock."

When the front door had closed upon Hex Mr. Sluis unfolded his plans.

"I haf already been in communication mit Scotland Yard," he said, "and I find I can prosecute this fine fellow for obtaining money by a trick. To-morrow you shall be here, my friendts, also the good Inspector Smith will be dressed like one of us, and we will teach this philanthropist a good lesson."

Mr. Sluis was a born organiser. On the following afternoon the secretary of Mr. Sluis drew from the bank the sum of £6,000 in sixty notes of £100 each. The numbers were carefully taken and marked under the supervision of Inspector Smith, and all was ready for the discomfiture of Captain Hex when he arrived that evening, accompanied on this occasion by his bodyguard.

He introduced the embarrassed Belshazzar to the assembled company. The moment he came in he recognised the atmosphere of hostility, sensed danger as a pointer scents game, but he was not greatly perturbed.

"Here we are, Captain Hex. Let me introduce you to my friends. Mr. Julius Bloomstein, of whom you have heard, another subscriber to your little scheme, eh?"

"It is very likely," said Hex, taking a good view of a gentleman who controlled quite a number of metal companies in England.

"This is Mr. Van Richter."

Hex bowed to the second.

"And this," indicating a severe-looking man, severely dressed, and unmistakably a police official, "is Mr. Tom Jones, from Liverpool."

"Glad to meet you, Mr. Tom Jones, from Liverpool," said Captain Hex, his eyes twinkling.

"And now," said Mr. Sluis, "to business. You have the jewels?"

Hex took the case from under his arm and flicked it open.

"Very good. They look splendid."

"You have the money?" asked Hex Mr. Sluis pulled open a drawer of his desk, took out the notes, and threw them on the desk.

"Count them," he said.

Hex went over them with the rapidity of a bank cashier.

"Correct," he said.

"Here is a pen and paper, Captain Hex," said Mr. Sluis. "You will please write at my dictation."

Hex took up the pen.

"Are you ready?"

He nodded.

"Received from Mr. Montague Sluis," dictated that gentleman, "the sum of £6,000 in payment for one string of pearls— you had better put genuine pearls," said Mr. Sluis airily, and Hex obeyed—"which I certify," continued Mr. Sluis, "are my property. Have you got that?"

"Yes," said Hex.

"Now, sign it."

The other signed in a large hand, "Reginald Hex," and put the date. He picked up the money and put it into his pocket, and suddenly the smile on the face of Mr. Sluis faded.

"That's all," he said quietly. "Inspector, you will do your duty."

Inspector Smith stepped forward.

"Do you charge this man?" he said.

"I charge him," said Mr. Sluis, reciting the formula which he had committed to memory, "with obtaining £6,000 by means of a trick and with defrauding me by selling artificial pearls as real."

"You have heard the charge," said the inspector. "You had better not say anything now. I shall take you down to Bow Street."

"You do so at your own risk, inspector," said Hex. "I suppose you are an inspector."

"My name is Inspector Smith, of Scotland Yard."

Hex nodded.

"I repeat that you will take me at your own risk," he said. "In the first place there has been no trickery. I sold this man the pearls for a price. I have given him the receipt, and I have the cash in my pocket."

"Persian pearls, my friend, Persian pearls," smirked Mr. Sluis. "I purchase genuine pearls."

"Of course you did," said Captain Hex. "Surely a connoisseur like yourself can distinguish between the artificial and the real."

He took a note-book from his pocket, and produced a printed bill, which was stamped and receipted.

"I bought these from Tiffanys in Regent Street," Hex went on. "There is the receipt for them, £2,000."

Mr. Sluis went pale.

"If you can prove that I have been defrauded," said Hex virtuously, "that I have purchased artificial pearls, I shall be awfully glad, because naturally I shall have an action against Tiffany."

"Real pearls!" gasped Mr. Sluis.

He picked up the necklace with a trembling hand, and carried it to the light. Long and earnestly he looked, then came back and laid his purchase on the table.

"Are they real, sir?" asked the Inspector.

Mr. Sluis could not trust himself to speak. He nodded. The inspector smiled.

"Well, of course, sir, you have no action against this gentleman."

"But they are not worth more than £2,000, and I have paid £6,000."

The inspector shrugged his shoulders.

"I am afraid that's your lookout, sir," he said.

"But I have paid £4,000 too much," insisted Mr. Sluis tremulously.

Hex laughed, thrust his hands into his pocket, and crackled the notes.

"That is exactly the amount I intended you to pay," he said. "If you hadn't been such a hog and hadn't been so keen on catching me you might have gone through the formality of examining the pearls and seen they were genuine."

"But you bought artificial pearls," said the agitated man. "You were seen to purchase them."

"Quite true," said Hex, "but I bought the real ones after I showed you the 'duds.'"

"For why did you buy these if not to defraud me?" bleated Sluis.

"I bought those," said Captain Hex as he made his way to the door, "to wear at your next party. Now, be sure you 'infite' me."

Captain Hex pulled off his gloves, descended from behind the steering wheel, and made a brief examination of his car. His companion, a tall, solemn, ex-soldier, watched the inspection with a doleful face.

Presently Captain Hex looked up.

"Belshazzar Smith," he said accusingly, "you didn't put the water in the tank."

"Didn't I, sir?" said Belshazzar Smith.

"What the dickens is the good of saying 'Didn't I, sir?' when you jolly well know you didn't!" said the indignant Captain Hex.

He looked round. Fortunately the car had stopped within a dozen paces of a small house that stood at the end of the village—a neat, white house of quaint architecture, with a glimpse through the ordered hedge of rosery and croquet-lawn and plethoric kitchen-garden.

"Go and borrow a pail of water," said Captain Hex. "No, stay; I'll go."

He walked to the little oak gate, up the wide gravel path, and pressed the electric button by the side of the door. Presently the door opened, and Hex took off his cap, for the pretty lady with sad, grave eyes who stood surveying him was obviously not the servant.

"I am so sorry to bother you, but my car has given out, and I wondered if you would be kind enough to let me have a pail of water," he said.

She smiled.

"I'm afraid I shall have to ask you to get it yourself," she said; "my servant is out. Will you follow me?"

She led the way through the parquetted hall to the neatest of kitchens. He found a bucket and filled it, replenished his car, and returned the vessel.

He waited in the hall to thank her, for she had disappeared when he returned, and was surprised when she came from the dining-room bearing a cup of fragrant tea.

"I am sure you will appreciate this," she smiled. "It is a very cold day."

She looked at the badge on his coat.

"You are a service man!"

"I was," he corrected.

She nodded.

The smile had faded from her face.

"My husband was a soldier," she said quietly.

He had noticed that she was in black, and through the open door of the dining room he saw suspended above the fireplace a sword in a glass case.

"West Sussex," she said. "He was killed on the Somme."

"Bad luck," said Hex, and she nodded again, biting her lip, and looking past him down the path. Then suddenly—

"You are not Captain Hex, are you?" she asked.

He looked at her in surprise,

"That is my name," he said.

"I am so glad to meet you." She put out her hand impulsively. "They tell me you are settling soldiers' families in the village. I think it's splendid of you."

Captain Hex was not easily embarrassed, but now he went a deep red.

"Yes," he said awkwardly; "I am bringing down twenty or thirty families. You see," he went on hurriedly, "it's not my money; at least it's money I have the absolute disposal of, but it's not mine. It's my pet scheme to do something for the soldier's widow and for the disabled man, and some little time ago I got £8,000 from a gentleman—well, not exactly a gentleman; he's a profiteer—and Belshazzar Smith and I— yes, the name is a bit startling, isn't it?" He smiled quickly. "He's my servant; well, he's not exactly my servant—"

"What a mass of contradictions you are," she laughed. "Won't you come in and tell me about it, and would your Belshazzar Smith like a cup of tea?"

"I'll call him," said Hex eagerly.

He went to the door and whistled, and the girl behind him laughed again, but softly and to herself. There was something immensely boyish about Captain Hex in his unguarded moments—a frankness and freshness that at any rate appealed to her.

Belshazzar Smith duly came, saluted the lady, and accepted the cup of tea with that embarrassment which all big men show in such circumstances.

"You are doing work you ought to very proud of," she said. Then she stopped, eyeing him thoughtfully. "I wonder," she said, half to herself, then flushed pink.

"Say what you were going to say," he encouraged her.

She shook her head.

"No, no," she said hurriedly. "It was only just a thought I had. I was wishing that there was some kind of institute or some kind of society, something that a man like you was directing, where we women could go with our little troubles. That's selfish, isn't it?" she laughed. "But the officer's widow is in rather a difficult position. She hates people doing nice things for her, and her troubles, as a rule, are so much more complicated."

"Mrs—?"

"My name is Willoughby," she said. "I am so sorry. I should have introduced myself before."

"Mrs Willoughby," he said earnestly, "it isn't only the Tommies I want to help, it is the wives and children of all the good comrades I have had. You don't know how I'd like to help. I know," he said hastily, stopping her protest, "I know it is not money you want or anything horrid like that, though it probably comes down to money," he laughed. "Most things do, don't they? Won't you tell me?"

She got up and paced the room, her hands clasped behind her.

"I think I will," she said after a while. "I am just aching to tell somebody, and there's nobody in the world that I can tell. It's about this house. My husband was an officer in the regular army, one of the old 'contemptibles,' you know," she said with a proud light in her eyes, "and the dearest and best of fellows. He had a small private income, and out of that we bought this house. When I say we bought it," she amended. "I mean my husband paid for it in instalments. There was one instalment due when he was killed. The house was purchased from a man who is very rich, and has a lot of house property in this county, but all the business was done through his agent, a man named Witte. About a month before my husband died Witte absconded. He had apparently been swindling his employer, and when I went down to pay his successor the last instalment I met the owner." She stopped and pressed her lips together as at some unpleasant memory.

"Well?" asked Hex curiously.

She shrugged her shoulders.

"The owner simply said that it was not one instalment that was due, but five—that is to say, about £600. There was no trace of any previous sum having been received."

"But surely you can trace the cheques?"

The girl shook her head.

"Mr. Witte used to ask my husband as a personal favour to pay him in cash."

"But the receipts?"

"That is the awful part of it," said the girl. "There are no receipts. My husband was, like many other soldiers, a very indifferent business man. He never bothered about receipts. He would carry them about in his pocket until they were worn through, and then he would throw them into the fire with the other debris he took from his pocket. There are some men like that," she smiled. "You see, Frank was too large and too generous and too trustful."

"I see," said Captain Hex.

"I think I made a mistake in saying I hadn't the receipts, because he was at first very nice and respectful and made no difficulty about the matter at all. It was when be asked me if I had the receipts and I told him I had none that he was so horrid."

"Very horrid?" said Hex.

She nodded.

"What is the name of your landlord?"

"Mr. Montague Flake."

Hex jumped up so quickly that he nearly upset the teacup he was holding in his hand.

"Montague Flake?"

His eyes were bright, and his white teeth showed in a delighted grin.

"What! King Montague of Margarinia!"

She smiled.

He reached town in the evening, and till late in the night he sat debating various schemes. In the morning be drove down to Leadenhall Street, where is situate the palatial offices of the U.P. Stores, Limited, of which Mr. Montague Flake was managing director and chairman.

"Yes, Mr. Flake had arrived," the clerk told him. "Had he a card? More important, had he an appointment?"

"I have neither card nor appointment. But will you tell him that a gentleman from the Treasury wishes to see him alone on most urgent private affairs?"

In ten seconds Hex was ushered to the presence. He entered sideways, instantly turned his back upon the figure at the desk, and looked meaningly at the clerk who had shown him in.

"You may go, Johnson," said the voice of Mr. Montague Flake, and when the door had closed Captain Hex turned.

For a moment, in fact until he was standing by the desk, the financier did not recognise one who only a few weeks before had, in the language of the law, "obtained by a trick" the sum of £8,000. When he did recognise the visitor Mr. Flake fell back in his chair in speechless, open-mouthed indignation.

"What, what, you!" he spluttered.

"Calm yourself," said Captain Hex, with a magnificent gesture, "don't forget your kingly dignity. I have come to speak to you on a matter of the gravest importance."

"Why, you scoundrel!" roared Mr. Flake, "you swindler! You obtained entrance to this room under false pretences. By Heavens! sir! I'll have you arrested! You said you were from the Treasury!"

"Quite right," said Captain Hex suavely, "wouldn't you call me a treasury? Haven't I got £8,000 of yours?"

Mr. Montague Flake jerked violently to his feet and reached for the bell.

"Before you press that bell," said Captain Hex solemnly, "consider!"

"I consider you a villain and a thief," said the wrathful man.

"Consider," said Captain Hex, "have you never heard of conscience? Have you never read in the papers that the Chancellor of the Exchequer has received fabulous sums from X.Y.Z. and A.B.C. in the form of conscience money? Do you not take account of the contrite heart and the repentant sinner?"

Mr. Flake was suddenly calm.

"H'm," he grunted, "of course, if you have come to make restitution, though, mind you, it was a low trick you played, but if you have come to disgorge your ill-gotten gains, I might have something else to say."

"Let me ease your mind," said Captain Hex, "I haven't come to do anything so silly. If you will sit down and will listen to me for a few minutes I think I can save you from—well something unpleasant."

Mr. Montague Flake looked at him.

"What do you mean?" he asked suspiciously.

"Doubtless in your life," said Captain Hex, "there have been incidents and episodes which you are anxious to forget."

The millionaire eyed him keenly, and there was in his eyes a sudden look of apprehension, which the other did not fail to mark.

"Oh," he growled, and settled himself into his chair with a shrug of his shoulders, "so that's the game is it? Blackmail!"

"You may call it blackmail," said Captain Hex, "or you may call it reparation. I am not particular what you call it."

He put his hat upon the table, laid his stick lengthwise (Mr. Montague Flake was too far gone to protest), wheeled up the easiest chair he could find, and sank into it in the graceful attitude of a man who had complete command of the situation.

Belshazzar Smith's Testimony

"I have in my pocket a little packet of documents which it is not my intention to show for the moment. It concerns—"

"Blackmail, eh?" said Mr. Montague Flake, and breathed with difficulty.

"It's an ugly word," said Captain Hex, "which I, as a man who has held the King's commission, do not like to hear applied to myself. But the matter is rather too serious—so serious that I am reluctant, very reluctant, to see the matter discussed in the press."

Mr. Flake opened his mouth, but said nothing. His steely eyes never left the face of his visitor.

"Before I proceed any farther," said Captain Hex, "I would like you to summon my servant, Mr. Belshazzar Smith, whom you have met before. He was the landlord of a cottage near Little Wenson, which you purchased at a price much above its market value."

"Because you had insinuated a swindling document into some manuscripts I had bought," interjected Mr. Flake violently.

"Because you found or thought you found a document describing the place where some treasure was hidden, and the place happened to be on this property. So you paid £8,000 for a cottage worth about £200. believing you were going to make a handsome and illicit profit."

"What do you mean, illicit? It was all fair and above board," protested Mr. Flake angrily.

"There is such a thing in Britain as the law of Treasure Trove," explained Captain Hex, "by which the State takes a large proportion of any hidden treasure found in the ground. Whether you had notified the Government that these precious stones were there or not I do not know."

The margarine king was silent.

"What do you want your man in for?"

Captain Hex shrugged his shoulders.

"You can have him or not as you wish," he said indifferently, "but I think it would make matters much more simple if you had him."

Mr. Flake hesitated a moment, then reached out and pressed the bell.

"Where is the man?" he asked gruffly, when the clerk appeared in answer to the summons.

"You will find him outside," said Captain Hex, not shifting his position of ease, "a tall man, in a pepper and salt suit, and an outrageous pink tie. He answers to the name of Belshazzar Smith, but you had better call him Mr. Smith, as he is rather sensitive."

Belshazzar strode into the room truculently, expecting trouble, but the atmosphere was extraordinarily calm.

"Come here, Belshazzar Smith," said Captain Hex, and pulled a little wad of paper from his pocket. He turned down the ends of two or three, and then he pointed.

"We will name no names," he said, with an inclination of his head to the watchful Flake.

"Do you know this person?" He pointed to something written on the paper. "When did you see that person last?"

"Yesterday," said Belshazzar Smith.

"Did that person make a certain statement to me in your presence?"

"Yes, sir," said Belshazzar Smith.

"That is all I ask. You may go, Belshazzar. I will rejoin you in a few moments."

Mr. Flake Explains

"Blackmail, eh!" said Mr. Flake for the third time.

"You are not very original," said Captain Hex. "This is not exactly blackmail."

"Which one is it?" he asked suddenly.

"We will name no names," said Captain Hex calmly.

"What do you want me to do?" asked Mr. Flake.

"You own a house called 'Rosemead;' when I say you own the house it is really the property of a widow of a brother officer. You are now trying to swindle her out of that house and—"

"It's a lie," said Mr. Flake loudly.

"You must not say that," said Hex, and his voice was sharp and menacing. "You can say what you like about me, but you must not give the lie to a lady who, as I have already told you, is the widow of a man who has fallen in this war to defend you and your like."

"Since you know all about it," said Flake, "you know that my agent absconded. I have reason to believe that he favoured this Captain Willoughby, and that Willoughby never paid him the instalments which were due on the house. There are no receipts, no records in the ledger."

"All this I grant," said Hex. "At the same time, you know in your heart of hearts that Willoughby paid. He was the soul of honour. If he hadn't paid he would have written excusing himself. If you can produce such a letter the matter need not go any further."

Mr. Flake was silent.

"I see you cannot, and under those circumstances I must ask you to give me a receipt in full for the missing five payments."

"I will see you in—"

Hex rose from his chair.

"I am not going to press this matter. I am not in a hurry." He waved his hand airily. "I will call back to-morrow at about this time. You can see me or not as you wish."

Mr. Flake made no reply, and with a little nod Captain Hex strolled from the apartment.

He looked at his watch. It was half-past twelve. He had telegraphed the night before to the girl to lunch with him in London. He had done this on the impulse of the moment before his plans were fixed, or indeed before he had any plans at all, and he wondered with just a little pang of uncomfort what she would say when he told her what had happened.

He found her waiting for him in the vestibule of Princes', a slender, girlish figure, more lovely than he had thought.

"I have got all sorts of confessions to make to you," he said ruefully when they had taken their places at the table.

"Have you—done anything?" she asked.

Briefly he described the interview, and was dismayed when he saw her face drop.

"Oh, but you shouldn't have done that, Captain Hex," she said. "I wouldn't have that happen. It isn't right that pressure should be put upon a man. I know you meant it kindly." And then her curiosity overcame her feeling of distress. "What dreadful thing has he done?" she asked. "Don't tell me if it is too awful."

Hex laughed. The sheer joke of it was too much for him.

"That's the funny thing," he said; "I don't know what he's done."

"You don't know what he's done!" she said in amazement.

He shook his head.

"All I know is that he is a man of 55, a very secretive man, very unscrupulous, and probably with a particularly tough past. You don't know what wretched souls he has pulled into the gutter. When I went to him I knew there must be something in his life, some sin darker than another."

"But—but the names that were on your paper?" she asked.

"It was the name of my landlord, who had collected the rent the day before," said Captain Hex calmly.

"Aren't you running risks?" she asked anxiously. "I would never forgive myself if you got into trouble over me."

"Don't worry about that," he said. "I am not blackmailing Montague Flake; he is blackmailing himself."

She was staying in town that night with an aunt, and promised to delay her return until the business had been settled one way or the other. It so happened that she had not long to wait.

That afternoon when Captain Hex returned to his office he found Belshazzar Smith in a state of suppressed excitement.

"He's rung up, sir," he whispered.

Belshazzar's attitude of secrecy, though there was nobody in earshot, in all matters pertaining to the business of the "firm" was very precious to Hex, but on this occasion he was too interested in the news.

"Who has rung up?" he asked.

"Flakie," whispered Belshazzar Smith excitedly. "He wants you to go down and see him at once. As 'Errick says—"

"Tell me about Herrick when I get back," said Captain Hex, and was half way down the stairs before Mr. Smith finished the interrupted quotation.

Hex was shown immediately into the big boardroom where Montague Flake sat, but it was a different Montague Flake to the harsh, self-satisfied man he had left that morning.

"Here is your receipt," he said, pushing a slip of paper across the table, "and here is the conveyance of the house. I don't know what your intentions are, Captain Hex," he said, and there was none of the old harsh, domineering quality in his voice, "but as I suppose you have been an officer you are going to behave like a gentleman. Although you have made no promise, I take it that you can settle this matter with the person concerned. How much does she want?"

Hex shook his head.

"Nothing more," he said firmly. "The matter is settled, and you will not hear of it again."

He wondered what the matter was. He could not even hazard a guess, and was terribly tempted to ask. Flake looked at him in astonishment.

"Are you sure that no money is wanted?"

"Absolutely sure," said Captain Hex firmly. "She does not wish to see you again."

"To see me?" said Mr. Flake. "What do you mean? She never knew me; I never met her."

"As she knew you by hearsay," continued Captain Hex hastily, realising he was on the wrong track.

"I suppose she did. You can tell her," he went on. "that her husband was not to blame in the matter at all, and that he died an honest man. Since you know all about it," he continued dejectedly, "I might well tell you that it was I who killed Witte, though it was done purely in self-defence. Her husband did not know this, and if had been charged with the murder he could not have defended himself."

"Good lor'," said Hex to himself.

"If Witte had lived he would have ruined me. One night he came over to this house and threatened me—threatened to expose me unless I handed over practically all my wealth to him. I did not know what to do. I told him to wait a moment, and I rang up Willoughby. Willoughby held most of the shares in a diamond company we were floating—a bogus company, though Willoughby did not know it—and I thought he might be able to help me. Willoughby came over, and Witte quietened down when he saw him. Afterwards the pair left the house and I followed them. Witte must have spotted me, for he made an excuse to leave Willoughby, and went off down a quiet side road. I followed, and he turned and confronted me.

"What happened," continued Flake I shakily, "I scarcely know. But I left him lying in the middle of the street. He tried to strike me, and I must have struck him back. In the darkness a motor ran over him, and it was taken to be an accident. That is how it happened."

"Good lor'!" repeated Hex to himself.

"You know, Captain Hex, I am glad it is all over now, and that I have been able to speak about it. It has so preyed on my mind that I couldn't sleep at night for thinking about it. At first I thought she knew nothing at all about it. But if she will let me I will make any compensation she wishes."

"She wants nothing else but to forget you," said Hex.

He was mopping his brow as he sped home along the Embankment.

"Whoever would have thought it of old Flakie," he mused. "And who would have thought he would have betrayed himself like that?"

CHAPTER VI

"'Gather ye rosebuds while ye may,'" said Belshazzar Smith poetically, "'old Time is still a flying, and this same flower that smiles to-day to-morrow will be dying.' 'Errick wrote that."

"He might have been doing something better," said Captain Hex. "Anyway, flowers don't smile—not Boliviski's flowers."

He and Belshazzar Smith were sitting on their favourite seat in the Temple Gardens, green and lively at this period of the year, and densely populated with lunch-hour loungers.

"'Errick says—" began Mr. Smith.

"Let's leave 'Errick alone," smiled Hex. "That poor man must turn in his grave twenty times a day. The thing we have to consider is not 'Errick's flowers or even Mr. Boliviski's roses, but Mr. Boliviski's surplus profits and how much he is going to devote of same to the promotion and upkeep of our Sailors' and Soldiers' Poultry Farm."

"He's a very close man," said Belshazzar Smith, puffing thoughtfully at his briar pipe, "a very close man indeed. His servants say that he weighs the bread he gives them, and measures the milk three times a day—and him worth millions."

"Officially he is not worth millions," said Hex. "When I went to him for a subscription he told me that the war had hit him very hard." He looked at his watch. "Wait for me here," he said, rising. "Boliviski has invited me to coffee. He nearly invited me to lunch, but thought better of it, and asked me to come in to the Savoy and meet him in the lounge."

He left Belshazzar basking in the spring sunlight, the picture of a contented man, and made his way to the Savoy.

Mr. Boliviski, a stout, red-faced man, with a heavy black moustache and side-whiskers, rose stertorously and offered a large, soft, limp hand.

"Ah. Captain," he wheezed, "what an unlucky fellow you are! I've just finished my coffee. Now, shall I order you some? Say the word and you shall have the best cup of coffee that the house can produce. Would you like a nice cigar? I see that you're a cigarette smoker. That's better, it doesn't cost so much. I don't smoke cigars myself, except now and again when a friend offers me one and I take it just to oblige him. Sit down, sit down, make yourself comfortable."

"From which I gather," said Hex, "that the chairs cost you nothing."

Mr. Boliviski chuckled.

"You will have your joke—but there are a lot of people like you in the city who think I'm a mean man. And there are a lot of people in the city who think I'm a rich man. But I'm not, Captain. I give you permission to go to the Surveyor of Taxes and ask him what my income is. He's a clever man, Captain Hex, as shrewd a man as there is in the city of London, and he's had accountants, real chartered accountants, the very best in the city of London, to examine my books and transactions, and he's never been able to trace a penny of excess profit."

He chuckled again, and it was the chuckle of a man who was enjoying a great joke all to himself.

"They say that you've done a big trade with Holland and made millions," said Hex.

Mr. Boliviski nodded delightedly.

"I know, I know," he said, "but where's their proof? They've examined my banking account— I gave 'em all the assistance I could, but they found no record. The truth is, Captain Hex, I did a little agency business, took a teeny-weeny commission— just a few pounds—and was satisfied. I don't hold with profiteering. When your country's at war, says I, don't try to crush the working classes, do all you can for 'em, help 'em over the stile, and you'll be respected. If the working classes knew what I've done for 'em, they'd put up a monument to me, they would indeed."

"Something in the shape of a guillotine," suggested Hex. "Now, I haven't come here to discuss your private affairs. I know you've made a lot of money."

How He Did It

Mr. Boliviski's hand went up in protest.

"Everybody knows it. The Income Tax Commissioners know it. You've simply dodged the authorities by making all your transactions cash transactions. You haven't taken cheques or given them. You've paid in bank notes, and you've received payment from other food profiteers in the same way."

"If I never get up from this seat—" began Mr. Boliviski.

"But you will get up from that seat," said Captain Hex. "You are going to behave like a fine old English gentleman; you're going to walk across to that writing table, produce your cheque book, and draw £6,000 from your bloated account to give men who have faced hell on your account a new start in life."

Mr. Boliviski shook his head slowly, and his face wore an expression of great pain.

"Oh, if I only could!" he said, with a melancholy intonation; "if I only could assist those poor dear fellows who have made what I might term sacrifices for democracy! But I can't, Captain Hex. I'm a poor man, and, beyond a few pounds at the bank, the goodwill of my provision business. and my little country cottage, I've nothing. You must come down and see my little place at Pilsham one of these days, Captain Hex. I've got some of the finest roses you ever saw—not expensive roses." he added hastily; "I don't hold with giving fancy prices for flowers."

"Quite right," said Captain Hex. "as 'Errick says—"

"Who's 'Errick?" asked Mr. Boliviski suspiciously.

"He's an income tax collector," replied Hex.

"Then you can tell him from me that he's a liar," said the stout man with some heat. "I've got no money to waste on da— on poor soldiers, and if I had I'd see 'em—I'd see 'em through any trouble they were in."

Captain Hex got up with a sigh.

"I see we shall have to employ other methods."

"Try 'em!" said Boliviski, no longer affable and obliging, but very truculent indeed. "Some of the cleverest fellers in the city of London have been after me, me lad, and they've all had to give me best. A young juggins like you ain't going to get over a man like me."

"What vulgarity!" murmured Hex.

"And as for your soldiers and sailors, let the country pay. What do we pay rates and taxes for, I'd like to know? Ain't there institootions for fellers that are hard up, and don't I pay poor rates, eh? You're not going to get a penny piece out of me, you and your £6,000!"

"It is now £10,000," said Captain Hex, "and you'll be lucky if it doesn't cost you more."

"Ha, ha!" said Mr. Boliviski with delicate sarcasm, "try it! You won't be the first person who has sneaked into my office and bribed my clerks. You won't be the first nosey parker that's buzzed round my safe deposit vault. You won't be the first person who's searched my house."

"You're quite right," said Captain Hex, "but I shall be the last, and when I have finished my investigations into your disgusting but furtive prosperity you will be sitting in a nice little six-by twelve cell at Wormwood Scrubbs, wishing that you had played the game with poor old Tommy."

Mr. Boliviski spluttered and flickered his hands in gestures appropriate to incoherent wrath, and Captain Hex went and rejoined his companion.

How the Land Lies

He spent the rest of the day making telephone inquiries. He had had a telephone installed in his sitting room, and found it very useful. A garrulous postmistress at Pilsham gave him a great deal of information of which he stood in need.

"I am going out of town to-morrow, Belshazzar," he said. "I have it in my mind that I am on the verge of a great discovery."

He went to Pilsham by the early train, inspected Mr. Boliviski's "little cottage," and by climbing a wall commanded an extensive view of the profiteer's demesne.

It was early for roses, but his imagination served him to visualise a picture of radiant beauty when June would come and these straight stems would be heavy with fragrant flowers. The cottage itself was a moderately large but unpretentious building, planned and executed in execrable taste. It was glaringly and patently new. Its face was smothered with stucco, it had porticos in the Corinthian style, and chimneys which were strikingly Elizabethan.

He went back to town very thoughtful, and on the following morning interviewed a bank manager who had also been a colonel before a sniper's bullet laid him out at Festubert.

Hex told his tale, and Mr. Martin listened with interest.

"You are up against a pretty tough proposition, Hex," he said. "We all know that Boliviski is a very rich man, but every effort to discover the extent of his wealth has been fruitless. Why, Somerset House has spent a small fortune in detectives and accountants to trace his profits, which I am certain have been enormous. The fact is, the artful old fox has not only confined himself to cash transactions, but that cash has been gold whenever he has sold to the neutral countries. We know this because a merchant in Amsterdam was shadowed from that city with £3,000 in guelder, and the money was traced to Boliviski. The old man must have got wind of the fact that he was being watched, and religiously recorded the transaction in his books, so that when the Inland Revenue people paid a surprise visit there was the money accounted for. He has a store somewhere, and if you can find it you will be doing the Government a good turn."

"Heaven forbid that I should assist the Inland Revenue in its nefarious work," said Captain Hex piously. "All I am anxious to get is a subscription of £10,000 to my new poultry farm. It's a wonderful place, my dear chap," he said enthusiastically, "and the Tommies are taking to it like ducks to water. With that £10,000 I'm going to build a new extension. I have had the offer of some land." And he went on to describe his scheme.

"Anyway," said the banker at last, "you won't get any money out of Boliviski. Why he's hoarding it, Heaven knows! I have naturally a constitutional dislike for all people who refuse to bank their money, but my dislike of Boliviski goes beyond this. He has done a lot to raise the price of commodities in this country, and he is raking in the money—for what? He has neither chick nor child, wife or relative. It is sheer greed—sheer lust of possession which animates the old devil."

Mr. Boliviski was in the habit of spending his week-ends at Pilsham. During the remainder of the week the house was in charge of an old housekeeper, who "slept out." He had a small staff of gardeners, who, however, were forbidden to touch the roses, and spent most of their time in the kitchen-garden, where he was able to raise vegetables with profit to himself.

He travelled down third class, and invariably walked the mile and a half between the station and his house. He regarded Saturday and Sunday as sacred to flora, and was not without reason annoyed on the Saturday morning when his slow-footed housekeeper came to him with a card inscribed, "Captain Hex."

"Tell him to go away. Tell him I don't want him here!" said Mr. Boliviski furiously. "If he won't go send for a policeman. I won't see him! I tell you I won't see him! Tell him to go to the devil—ah good morning, Captain Ilex!"

For Hex, who was nothing if not pushful, had followed the messenger.

"I thought I'd come down and see those roses you were boasting about," said Hex. "I can stay to lunch and catch the first train back after."

"There's a good train before lunch," growled Mr. Boliviski.

"I don't particularly want a good train." said Hex; "in fact, the good points of a train don't worry me a cent."

"Well, what do you want?"

Mr. Boliviski faced him squarely. He was dressed in his oldest suit. On his hands were leather gardening gloves, and in one of them a murderous looking pair of shears.

"We were talking the other day," said Hex, "about the £10,000 you were anxious to devote to my philanthropic scheme."

"Ten thousand cats!" spluttered Mr. Boliviski. "I'll see you—"

"Yes, yes, yes," said Captain Hex, "I know where you will see me. But I really am in need of this money, and I think you would save yourself a great deal of trouble if you paid up. You see. I happen to know something about your little nest egg."

The stout man's eyes narrowed.

"Oh, you do, do you?" he said slowly. "Now, man to man and with no witnesses present, I'll call your bluff. You tell me where my little nest egg is to be found, and I'll give you your £10,000."

"What time do you lunch?"

"I don't lunch and I won't lunch!" exploded Mr. Boliviski. "There's a village policeman here, my friend, and I'll have you off the premises in two twinks!"

"Do anything you like," said Hex, "but don't call me your friend. People who don't know me might be deceived into believing you."

He left by the goods train that went before lunch.

That night he outlined his plan to Belshazzar Smith.

"The money's as good as in my pocket," he said, "though it worries me."

"Worry," said Belshazzar Smith, "is the unconscious—"

"Yes, yes, I know, 'Errick," said Hex. "This is rather serious. Ought I to ask him for £10,000 or £20,000?"

"Find out what he's got and take half," said Belshazzar Smith.

"That is a bright idea," agreed his partner.

The real difficulty, as Hex knew and had known all along, was to find the architect who had designed Boliviski's house. Pilsham only knew him as "a foreigner," a dour, reticent man, presumably a Dutchman, since most of the workmen were Dutch, and had been imported in the year before the war to construct

Mr. Boliviski's country house. It was this fact which had put Hex upon the trail. Boliviski was not the kind of man to go to the trouble of importing large bodies of labourers and artisans from Holland if it cost money, as undoubtedly it would cost. Why, then, had he taken this unusual step, unless it was to prevent the details of the house and its construction becoming public property?

To his surprise he had discovered, by making judicious inquiries, that the general lay-out of the house was fairly well known to the villagers. Various women and men had been up to "The Nid," as Mr. Boliviski's romantic fancy had christened it, and as cleaners or repairers of windows, bells etc., had penetrated to every corner, even to Mr. Boliviski's study.

"The thing to do, of course, is to find the architect, and that's going to be rather a job," said Hex, after he had explained his plan. "The only thing we know about him is that he stayed at the Adlin Hotel in London, and occasionally visited the works whilst they were in progress."

He consulted a paper which he took from his pocket.

"I find that the first job done was the building of the wall. Obviously this was because the architect did not wish to be overlooked whilst the house was in course of construction."

"Send him a letter," said Belshazzar Smith. "Send him a registered letter and pay for an acknowledgment. That's what we used to do in a debt-collecting agency I was connected with. The letter, forwarded to the gent, and the receipt comes back to you with his name and address on it."

Hex looked at him admiringly.

"There's a great deal of talent lost in you," he said; "but will you kindly tell me where I should send the letter?"

"To the last place you heard from him."

Hex nodded.

"I'll go to the hotel. It will save time," he said.

He was gone all the afternoon, but returned in triumph.

"Hans van Rhyn is in London, my lad," he said cheerfully. "He has come over on an official mission on behalf of the Dutch Government—it has something to do with the shipping of building material. I have an appointment with him at seven o'clock."

"The money is yours," said the confident Belshazzar.

Mr. Hans van Rhyn was a gristled little man, who spoke good English when he spoke at all, but on the whole was a most excellent listener.

This Hex discovered in the first five minutes of their conversation, and very wisely adapted his tactics to Mr. Van Rhyn's temperament.

"I am afraid," said Mr. Van Rhyn, "that I cannot oblige you because I am not here on business, and really I have no desire to do any more business in this country. My experience has not been a very pleasant one, and I vowed I would never again undertake a contract in this country."

"I am profoundly sorry to hear this," said Hex regretfully, "because you are the only man who can carry out the work which I want doing."

The Dutchman looked interested.

"I want a house built," said Captain Hex slowly, " and I want it built exactly on the same lines as the one you built for Mr. Boliviski."

A frown gathered on the other's face.

"That is an undertaking which I do not care to have anything to do with," he said shortly. "Your friend Mr. Boliviski—"

"He is not my friend," said Hex hastily. "He is merely an acquaintance."

Still the Dutchman shook his head.

"It is not work I care to do," he said "even if you are not a friend of Mr. Boliviski."

"I assure you I am not that," said Hex, now sure of his ground. "I regard Mr. Boliviski as the meanest, most miserable creature on the face of the earth."

The Dutchman nodded, and his taciturn face lit up with a smile.

"I am almost inclined to do it for you but really it is impossible. Why do you want a house of that character?" he asked suddenly. "Are you a wine connoisseur too?"

"Yes," said Hex quietly.

"In that case," said Van Rhyn, "you can get any architect to design a house unless you are eccentric and believe that people are trying to rob you of your wine. I don't know much about wine," he went on, "but I know that it keeps just as well in an ordinary cellar as in a vault."

"Away from the house?" murmured Hex.

"Exactly," said the Dutchman. "I have always thought Mr. Boliviski's idea fantastic."

They talked together for an hour, and parted the best of friends. Mr. Van Rhyn steadfastly refusing to indicate approximately the plan of Boliviski's house and outdwellings.

Belshazzar Smith accompanied him to Pilsham the next morning, and they found lodgings in the village. That night, armed with a sword-cane, Hex climbed the forbidding wall of "The Nid"—the gate was securely locked—and began his investigations.

A sword-cane is an admirable probe, and, throughout the night, the two men systematically tested the beautiful rose garden of Mr. Boliviski. It was just before dawn when Hex, thrusting his sword into the earth, felt the point grate against something hard. Feverishly they cleared away the mould with a garden-trowel which Smith had brought, and in a few minutes had scraped clear a square foot of concrete facing.

Captain Hex replaced the earth, and he was very thoughtful on his way back to the village.

"That is the place all right," he said, "a little concrete house built underground, and probably entered through a trap in the roof. Now, Belshazzar, we're up against it. What are we going to do?"

"Do?" said the astonished Belshazzar Smith, "why, of course, we'll go and take it."

"Would you commit a robbery?" asked Captain Hex shocked.

"Why not?" said the unemotional Belshazzar.

"For many reasons," replied Hex seriously. "If we expose this man we don't get any money. If we take our share and leave him the rest we condone his crime. If we tell him we know the money is there, and ask for our little lot we are guilty of blackmail, besides giving him an opportunity of getting the stuff away. There is only one thing for it, Belshazzar."

"What's that?" asked Belshazzar.

"You've got to die," said Captain Hex.

"Oh!" said Belshazzar blankly.

"You've got to be murdered," said Hex.

Mr. Smith looked at him uneasily.

Of these conversations Mr. Boliviski was, of course, ignorant, but he had not been in his house very long on his return to the country that Saturday before he knew that there were unpleasant visitors in the village. He was, therefore, not surprised, except in one respect, to see Captain Hex walking across the garden to where he was standing, pruner in hand.

"How did you get in?" he demanded. "I gave strict instructions that you weren't to be admitted."

"That's all right," said Hex listlessly. "I got over the wall."

Mr. Boliviski looked at the intruder curiously. Captain Hex was not his jovial self. His tone was sad, his demeanour was dejected, and he wore a black tie and a deep band of black about his left arm.

"I had to see you," said Hex. "After all, it concerns you more than anybody else."

"What's the game?" asked the suspicious Mr. Boliviski.

"I admit I was suspicious of you," said Hex, "and I have been down here three days searching for your hidden treasure house."

"You've got a cheek," said Mr. Boliviski, turning a shade paler nevertheless.

"I had an idea it was in this garden," Hex went on gloomily. "I had a dream that you had a little concrete vault built somewhere about here."

He waved his hand towards the rose trees, and Mr. Boliviski swallowed hard.

"Night after night," Hex went on, "my unfortunate companion and I have been probing this garden."

"Well, I'm d—d!" gasped Mr. Boliviski.

"I hope not," said the sad Hex. "As I was saying, night after night Belshazzar snd I searched in vain for your golden treasury. Belshazzar thought it was on one side of the garden; I thought it was on another. Two nights ago we quarrelled." He paused impressively.

"Well?" said Mr. Boliviski.

"I killed him," said Captain Hex simply. "I cut his throat. It was quite easy. I used a new knife that I'd bought in town. For eight-and-sixpence," he added.

Mr. Boliviski was staring with incredulous eyes.

"You murdered him!" he whispered hoarsely.

"Cut his throat," said Hex, "like that."

He made a gesture, and Mr. Boliviski leapt back.

"I have come to confess my crime."

"But, but," stammered Mr. Boliviski, "you're an infernal scoundrel, sir! To cut a man's throat in my garden! I'll have the police after you in a minute."

"Wait a moment," said Hex; "I not only killed him here, but I buried him here."

"Where?" Mr. Boliviski's voice was hardly audible.

"There!"

Hex pointed to ground which had evidently been recently disturbed.

"But you couldn't bury—"

Mr. Boliviski stopped short and bit his lip.

"I buried him there!" said Hex. "Send for the village constable; he has only to dig to prove my words."

The stout man's face went from red to white, from white to purple.

"Send for the village constable," moaned Hex. "Let me again face the victim of my crime!"

"How much do you want?" asked Mr. Boliviski with an effort.

"What is money? What is £20,000?"

"You said £8,000!" roared Boliviski savagely.

"What is a paltry £20,000? Will that ever wipe away the memory of this sad occurrence?"

"Now, look here," said Mr. Boliviski, "speaking as business man to business man, you've bitten me, and I'll pay. Come to my office on Monday morning."

"Send for the police," said Hex. "I can't wait till Monday."

"Suppose I gave you a cheque for £10,000?"

"Send for the police," said Hex in great distress.

"I'll give you the full amount," said Boliviski, and the words nearly choked him. "You've got me, and I know when I've been had."

"£20,000 to me, and the remainder to the Chancellor of the Exchequer, or it's a prison cell for one of us!"

Mr. Boliviski did not speak for a long time. And then he only sighed.

"Come into the house," he said at last.

CHAPTER VII

HOW MR. MILSON WREN WAS OUTWITTED

"I often wonder," said Belshazzar Smith, "what these 'ere profiteers do with their money. As 'Azlitt says, 'Money of itself is valueless.'"

"That's true, Belshazzar," said Captain Hex, "you can only eat one dinner at a time; you've only got one stomach. You can only sleep in one bed at a time, but also," he added thoughtfully, "it helps a philanthropic man who is anxious to subscribe large sums to military charities to do so without experiencing a sickening feeling in the pit of the stomach."

Belshazzar Smith nodded.

"Quite right, sir," he said, "the poultry farm, as 'Errick says—"

"It isn't the poultry farm, Belshazzar," corrected Captain Hex gravely; "that's on its legs now, thanks to the generosity of our dear friend. No, it is a larger and a much more important organisation which is in need of money at the present moment. If I had to write a school essay at this moment on Great Britain I should describe it as an island surrounded by super Dreadnoughts and populated by demobilised subalterns. At least that is how it strikes me. These boys are coming out of the army full of life, with faith in the future. They are drawing their gratuities and never having had so much money in all their lives, they are looking through the paint shops for the right kind of red wherewith to decorate this old town. At least that's the popular idea, Belshazzar Smith."

"I say that is the popular idea," continued Hex, lighting a fresh cigar; "but in reality the demobilised subaltern is looking round, not so much for trouble as for work. And it isn't only the subaltern. There's a fellow in the City whose office boy was a bright lad who was about to he promoted to a junior clerkship when the war broke out, enlisted straight away, and has come back a Brigadier-General. Well you can't put a Brigadier-General licking stamps, Belshazzar."

"It isn't likely," said the indignant Belshazzar, shivering at the thought of the sacrilege.

"And you can't put him running errands or entering up potty little books or doing any of that kind of work, Belshazzar," continued Captain Hex. "He's been doing man's work, and you've got to find a man's job for him. So I'm starting a big training school to fit these fellows for civil life—generals, colonels, majors, and subalterns—Belshazzar, who are as much in need of help, and more so, than you were when you left the army. This is going to cost a lot of money, but there's a lot of money lying loose in this world which I can find employment for. Now, have a good look at the Rogues' Gallery." He pointed to the wall whereon were displayed the photographs of sinful men. "Is there any likely-looking gentleman there who takes your eye, Belshazzar?"

"Well, I can't say that I'm struck on any of them," admitted Belshazzar, "but appearances is deceitful. As 'Errick says—"

"He's been talking about that, too, has he?" said Hex. "Does he give you any idea as to who our philanthropist is going to be?"

Belshazzar Smith thought for a moment, and then—

"He don't," he said decisively.

Hex strolled up and down the room, his hands in his pockets, his chin on his breast

"I rather fancy Mr. Milson Wren will head our subscription list," he said, "with £2,000."

Belshazzar Smith agreed. He did not know Mr. Milson Wren from any other kind of wren. He had not the slightest idea as to the financial standing of Mr. Milson Wren, or how large was the heart of that philanthropist. But he had supreme faith in Hex.

"Mr. Milson Wren, whose portrait does not appear in our collection," continued Hex, "is a gentleman who has made money out of motor-cars. He has made so much money that if he starts to write down his possessions he would get writer's cramp before he got to the end of them."

"He must be well off," said Belshazzar Smith.

"You've guessed it first time, Belshazzar," said the admiring Hex. "He's the victim."

Belshazzar nodded.

"Well, he won't mind parting with a little bit," he said cheerfully.

"On the contrary," retorted Hex, "he will mind very much. It is the man who has the money who hates parting with it. It is always the billionaire who counts his change, Belshazzar, as you will discover if you diligently search your 'Errick."

Mr. Milson Wren was, as everyone knows, an extremely rich man. Though, unlike Midas, everything he touched did not turn to gold, most of the things he dabbled in produced for his pocket greasy-looking bank notes of fabulous value. He ran motor-cars, ships, and coal, lead, copper, and spelter. He did his running from a very small office in Threadneedle Street, where he maintained two clerks and a small washstand, which, with a desk and a chair, constituted the furniture of his private office, and he grew in opulence, if not in beauty, day by day.

His was one of those mysterious businesses which is seen in every large city. The very poverty of his bureau advertised his wealth. In private life he lived magnificently in a flat in Park Lane, and entertained on a lavish scale at the best of the London hotels.

Hex wrote him a letter explaining the object of his new scheme, and received in reply a note so formal and discouraging that it might have been sent from the War Office itself:—

"Sir,— I am directed by Mr. Milson Wren to acknowledge receipt of your letter of even date, and in reply to inform you that Mr. Milson Wren regrets that owing to the many calls upon his private purse he is unable to accede to your request. Wishing you every success in your efforts to provide schools for demobilised officers, he is willing at some future date, if you care to approach him, and when your scheme is in running order, to be an annual subscriber to the extent of one guinea.—Very sincerely,

"J. BODEN, Secretary."

"It was the sort of answer I expected." said Hex. "I am going down to see old man Wren."

"Old man Wren" interviewed him in his shabby office, and "old man Wren" was a hard-faced man of forty-five, with no hair worth speaking about, a heavy black moustache, and a cold, brilliant eye which bore a permanent expression of suspicion.

Hex sized him up on their first meeting. This was a bully, overpowering, a loud and violent man. He flamed up at Hex as the latter entered his office.

"Can't you take 'No' for an answer?" he roared. "My secretary wrote to you and told you that I couldn't give you any subscription, and that ought to be enough for you. I've got something better to do than see people who are cadging."

"Elegantly put," said Hex, "and as to your having something better to do, why, I don t think that if you had got from now till Whitsun that you could think up a better occupation than putting your right hand in your trousers' pocket and producing the wherewithal to help forward the men who saved you from double damnation."

"Young man," said Mr. Wren noisily, "I'm going to humour you. I've done my bit in the war, and don't forget it! I've got £100,000 invested in War Loans. If you hadn't had money you wouldn't have been able to fight. Don't you realise that we people at home have done our bit?"

"And you're drawing five per cent, per annum on your bit," said Hex. "You're a sensible man, Mr. Wren—by-the-way, are you related to the gentleman who built St Paul's Cathedral?"

Mr. Wren choked.

"I see that you're not. Well, I'm going to put all my cards on the table. I know that you're a very wealthy man, and I have been told that you're a very charitable man."

"The man who told you that is a liar," growled Wren.

"Very possibly," said Hex. "I read it in the newspapers. I know that you made enormous sums out of manipulating the market."

"Another lie," said Wren, "and anyway it's no business of yours. What the devil do you mean by coming into my office and talking to me like this? By gad. I'll have you thrown out!"

"Don't," said Hex.

He thought a moment, and an idea flashed on him. Hex's great ideas invariably came that way.

"Well, perhaps you will," he added more mildly, "but before you do anything violent, Mr. Wren, I would only ask you is it not true that since the war broke out you have acquired large sums of money, and that you have purchased a big estate in Somerset, and that you are breaking into the county so to speak? I have seen your photographs in the illustrated weeklies hunting with the Somerset Hounds. I have read particulars of your subscriptions to the various county funds. Am I therefore mistaken in believing that you are trying to break into society?"

Mr. Wren went apoplectic.

"By heaven! By Gad!" he said. "Here, Johnson!" he yelled at the open door.

A weedy clerk came in, and he glared at Hex through his spectacles.

"Show this man out," gasped Mr. Wren. "Show him off the premises, Johnson."

"Wait, rash man," said Hex. "Remember that the British Army saved you—"

Mr. Wren interrupted him to pass a few remarks upon the British Army, which he consigned to places and in circumstances and conditions which it is unnecessary to record. Mr. Wren was a coarse man, despite his wealth, and his language was lurid.

"I expect to hear from your people in the next two or three days," and with that Captain Hex stepped lightly down the stairs and joined the waiting Belshazzar Smith.

"Did you get an idea?" asked Belshazzar anxiously, for Hex had gone into the building without any definite plan.

"A wonderful one," said Hex. "Come on home, Belshazzar. I shall want your assistance in planning out a series of brilliant outrages."

Now, though Milson Wren had neither chick nor child he had a large, important wife, on whom Providence had bestowed great opportunities for the display of jewels, particularly of large and lustrous pendants. She lived at Corley Court, a noble residential property which had come into the market during the war, and which had been acquired by Mr. Milson Wren as a general headquarters for his impending attack against the exclusive circles of Somerset society.

He looked forward to the day when he would be returned a member for the constituency, a very old and Conservative one, and would rise by approved and conventional degrees until the morning newspaper announced that "Mr. Milson Wren, M P., upon whom a peerage of the realm has been conferred, will be known as Lord Corley of Corley."

Hex spent two days dodging about the clubs making investigations.

"Wren's private reputation is more or less poisonous," he said to the interested Belshazzar Smith. "I find that he has been behind one or two theatrical enterprises, and that there has been an unsavoury episode or so in the past few years.

He retailed to the wide-eyed Mr. Smith particulars of those episodes.

"I didn't think he was that kind of fellow, sir," said Belshazzar, shaking his head, "and it's rather a pity he is. We can't tackle that sort of thing."

"No, my wise friend," said Hex; "you've got my whole scheme in your head. We can't blackmail the blackguard, and I wouldn't if I could."

"Do you think he'll summon you?"

"Not he," said Hex contemptuously. "We'll go down to Corley to-morrow, and we'll begin our great campaign."

The news that Captain Hex and his henchman had arrived in the small country town of Corley, and that they had taken up their residence at the Corley Arms, was duly reported to Mr. Wren.

"Who are these people, my dear?" asked his large wife at breakfast (at this hour she looked as though somebody had rubbed her face in a flour bin).

"Oh, a fellow named Hex," growled Wren. "It doesn't amount to anything. He is the man I was telling you about."

"The man that wanted £2,000!" gasped Mrs Wren.

"That's him," replied Wren grimly. "He had better not try any of his tricks down here, or, by the Lord, we'll show him something. He wanted me to subscribe to some water charity scheme of his, and, of course, I turned it down. There was no publicity in this thing, my dear, you understand."

She understood, and nodded.

"What's the good of putting money in a show like that, hey? Why, the papers wouldn't put a line about it. Besides, those London charities don't do me any good. If we've any money to chuck about we'll chuck it about down here. What do you say, Matilda?"

"That's my view absolutely," sad the lady, rolling a napkin with a dexterity born of practice. She was the daughter of a boarding-house keeper when Mr. Wren, in his shady days, had met her.

It appeared from the posters that were conspicuously displayed in the town that Captain Hex had come down to lecture on "What Britain Can Do for Her Demobilised Soldiers."

He had hired a hall, and the lecture was billed a week ahead. There were two flat stone pillars supporting the gates which opened on to the drive into Corley Court. They were just the right size on which a couple of double-crown posters could be displayed. Two such bills appeared one morning advertising the lecture, and were promptly torn down by Mr. Wren's orders. In the middle of the night somebody must have posted two more, because when Mr. Wren strolled down to the village in the morning he found them.

"We must watch to-night," said Mr. Wren after these posters had been duly removed, "and when the rascals post the bills we will nab them."

There followed telephone communication between him and the chief constable of the county, furtive visits paid by the local police sergeant, laboriously disguised in private clothes, and that night men watched and waited, none more impatiently than Mr. Wren, who desired to be present when the detection of the criminal was accomplished. They had not long to wait. Soon after eleven o'clock a dark form come along the road whistling cheerfully, carrying a small pot of paste in his hand, and scientifically affixed two new posters, one to each side of the gate.

Captain Hex "Caught"

They waited until he had finished, then leapt out at him.

"Now, my lad," said Wren, "I've got you. I'm going to make you pay for this."

"Good lad," said Hex cheerfully.

"Shall I tear the posters down?" said a policeman.

"Oh, no," replied Wren. "We shall want these as evidence. Leave them up. But to make sure that they are not pasted over. I have arranged to put a little mark on them. Brown, where is that pot of paint?"

A gardener loomed up out of the background with a pot of paint, and in the darkness Mr. Wren painted a big cross over the offending bills.

"I think we shall recognise that in the morning," he said.

"I fear that you will," said Hex. "What are you going to do with me?"

"I'm going to give you in charge."

"I'm afraid you can't," said Hex, with a little laugh. "The most you can do is to summon me—as usual."

"Is that so, sergeant?"

"That's so, sir," said the man. "You know you're not allowed to post bills on private property."

The first person to see the bills in the morning was Mr. Belshazzar Smith, who came at daylight and took a time-exposure photograph of them. The second person was the sergeant of police, who came to Mr. Wren with a troubled face.

"About that summons, sir, you want to take out against this man Hex."

"Well, what of it?" asked Wren.

"Well, sir," said the man, "I don't know whether it would be advisable to go on with it."

"Go on with it! Of course, I'm going on with it."

"Come and look at the picture, sir," said the police sergeant, and Mr. Wren in some perturbation walked down the drive and examined the disfigured bills.

He gasped. And well he might gasp, because these were not invitations to the lecture that Hex had posted, but two beautiful lithographs of a most august person. Mr. Wren's paintbrush had splashed across a Royal nose and had cut away and hideously disfigured a portion of a Royal beard.

"I don't think this ought to get out, sir," said the policeman. "The county is very exclusive, and they'd not like that at all. Besides, Captain Hex is a soldier, and he's speaking for soldiers, and that's not the sort of reputation you want down here, sir."

"Cover them up, tear them down!" spluttered Mr. Wren. "Don't go on with the summons. Curse him!"

Captain Hex heard the news (from the same police sergeant) that the prosecution was not being proceeded with, and nodded.

"I didn't think it would," he said. "He's a difficult old devil to deal with, and I really do not want to libel him seriously. I'll go up and see him."

Mr. Wren was officially not at home when Hex called.

Hex went back to his hotel, and returned to London.

"Do you see this fellow's idea," said Mr. Wren to his wife. "He wanted to get me into Court, blacken my name before the county, and ruin me socially."

"But you were too many for him," said his admiring wife.

"I rather think so," said Mr. Wren. "You know what I am. I can be led, but I can't be driven. That fellow's cancelled his lecture, and it's a very good thing. I happen to want the hall myself."

"Are you giving a lecture, Mill?" she asked in surprise.

He smiled.

"The Conservative Association have asked me to give my views to the public. I think I told you that there was some chance of my being elected when Chancery, the sitting member, is raised to the Peerage. Well, he's going to be in the next honours list, and I think it's very likely that I shall take his place."

She rose and, waddling round the table, kissed him on the brow.

"I always said you'd get on," she said.

"I always said so myself," remarked Mr. Wren. "I have just sent down to the printer the copy for the bill, and I'm going to engage all the hoardings to advertise the meeting."

To have his bill printed was one thing, to have it posted was another, as he discovered when his secretary returned with the amazing intelligence that every hoarding in Corley had been booked up for a month. Yet it was the off season when bill posters are least busy, and when space is to be had for a song.

"Booked up!" said Mr. Wren. "Then who's booked up the hoardings?"

"Captain Hex, sir," replied the secretary.

Mr. Wren's jaw dropped.

"What does he want it for?" he asked at last.

"He's got some scheme on, sir, and he's booked up all the posting space."

So Mr. Wren had to be content with bills displayed in sympathetic windows and with the few sandwich-men procurable in that small town.

What Hex was "up to" he was soon to learn. Driving down to the station a few days later, he found every hoarding smothered with large posters. They bore the simple inscription—"Who Did It?"

It was a lithographic enlargement of a poster depicting the head and shoulders of an august personage, suitably inscribed top and bottom with patriotic sentiments regarding the shield of the navy (it had originally been issued by the Navy League, Mr. Wren discovered afterwards), and across that respected face was drawn a large and ugly cross.

Mr. Wren stared and stared. He was not the only person staring. Sir John Benson, a local magnate, also on his way to the railway station, recognised his neighbour with a nod.

"What the dickens does that mean?" he asked. "What Bolshevik has been playing his game here?"

"I don't know," said Mr. Wren hastily. "I haven't the slightest idea."

It was not only on the hoardings of the town that the abominable reminder of Mr. Wren's unconscious disloyalty appeared. There were posters on the platform. There were posters on Charing Cross Station, and on a hoarding opposite Mr. Wren's office was the largest poster of all. Mr. Wren consulted his solicitor, and his solicitor sent to Captain Hex the kind of letter which a solicitor would write in the circumstances—it was full of vague and mysterious warnings as to the fate which would overtake the seeker after £2,000 subscriptions.

Two days later the letter in poster form, only the names of the writer, the addressee, and the interested client were omitted, appeared on the hoardings side by side with the "Who Did It?" sheet. It was headed, "Written on Behalf of the Man Who Did It."

"There's no sense in raving," said the philosophical man of law. "He has committed no offence, and anyway you have made a fool of yourself. You have got into the hands of a lawful blackmailer. What chance would you have of being elected for the Corley Division if it were known that yon had insulted Royalty?"

"But he made me say it," wailed the millionaire. "He almost put the words into my mouth!"

"What are you going to do?"

"Fight him! Every penny I have shall go in to ruin the rascal. Fight him, Peters! The fellow is notorious! He has swindled half a-dozen people I could name."

The interview took place in the solicitor's office. The lawyer was a man of the world. He was examining his cigar contemplatively.

"Mr. Wren," he said, "you have many irons in the fire, including a number of theatrical ventures."

"I have," said Mr. Wren a little surprised.

"And you know several theatrical people, including Miss Dorothy du Bonnet."

"A very charming girl," said Mr. Wren stoutly.

"Very," said the solicitor, "she came to see me to-day."

"Why?" asked the other in surprise.

"Well, it seems that you told her about this persecution of Hex's and that she was very indignant."

"Naturally," said Mr. Wren.

"And you gave her Hex's address?"

Mr. Wren shifted uneasily.

"What of it?" he asked.

"Well, she wrote a letter defending you," said the solicitor blandly; "she said how she had known you for years and years, what a kind man you were and that you were the dearest boy in the world. And when she had done it she came to ask me whether she had done right. Clients always do that sort of thing."

"You are quite sure she said 'dearest boy in the world?'" he said hollowly.

"Quite," replied the solicitor, "it will look well on a poster."

Mr. Wren sat down and wrote a cheque for £2,000, and might have saved himself the trouble, for an hour before this Hex was saying to Belshazzar Smith—"Of course, we can't use the lady's letter, Belshazzar. That wouldn't be playing the game. He is such a thick-skinned rascal that I don't know how we are going to get that money."

"What about laying in wait for him," said Belshazzar hopefully, "and chloroform him? 'Errick says that the unconscious mind—"

At that moment Mr. Wren's cheque arrived by special messenger.

Edgar Wallace – A Short Biography

Richard Horatio Edgar Wallace was born on the 1st April 1875 at 7 Ashburnham Grove, Greenwich. His mother, Mary Jane "Polly" Richards was born into an Irish Catholic family in Liverpool in 1843 and had worked in theatres, both as an actress in bit-parts and as a stagehand and usherette, until she married a Merchant Navy Captain, Joseph Richards, in 1867. He too had been born into an Irish Catholic family in Liverpool. His father had also been a Captain in the Merchant Navy, and his mother's family had a marine background. Mary was eight months pregnant with Joseph's child when he died at sea, and it was once the child had been born that she first turned to the stage, taking the stage name Polly Richards.

She joined the Marriott family theatre troupe in 1872. It was managed by Mrs. Alice Edgar, Richard Edgar, Grace Edgar, Adeline Edgar and Richard Horatio Edgar, Wallace's father. In late 1874 Mary and Richard Horatio Edgar had a brief sexual encounter at the party following a successful show, and she fell pregnant. Worried about the scandal which would ensue and fearing that she might forever lose her job at the troupe, she fabricated an obligation in Greenwich would detain her there for at least six months. She lived in a room in the boarding house on Ashburnham Grove until her son, Edgar, was born. She had already made preparations through her midwife for a couple to foster the child, and when Edgar was born the midwife presented her with Mrs Freeman. Her husband was a fishmonger at Billingsgate market and she already had ten children. She was happy to foster the child and for Polly to make frequent visits to see him in exchange for a small sum of money which Polly made from her work in the theatre troupe.

Wallace was now known as Richard Horatio Edgar Freeman, taking his father's forenames and his foster family's surname. Broadly speaking his childhood was a happy one. The Freemans looked after him lovingly and he had good friendships with his foster siblings, particularly Clara Freeman, twenty years his senior, who often looked after him as a child. After a few years Polly's finances tightened and she was no longer in a position to afford the fee she had been paying the Freemans. However, they had grown to love the young Wallace and opted to adopt him in order to keep him out of the workhouse. Polly could no longer visit him. George Freeman was keen to ensure that he had equal opportunities and did all he could to secure him an education at St. Alfege with St. Peter's, a Peckham boarding school. Despite his adoptive father's efforts, though, Wallace left the school aged twelve for truancy.

Instead he went to work and by the time he was fourteen or fifteen he had experience selling newspapers at Ludgate Circus, near Fleet Street, as a worker in a rubber factory, as a shoe shop assistant, as a milk delivery boy and as a ship's cook. He stole from the milk company which resulted in his dismissal, and in 1894 was engaged to a local girl from Deptford named Edith Anstree, though he broke this off and instead joined the Infantry. He adopted the name Edgar Wallace which he took from Lew Wallace, the author of Ben-Hur, and his medical record records a diminutive 33" chest and a stunted growth. his first posting was with the West Kent Regiment in South Africa in 1896, though he did not enjoy military life, arranging to be transferred to the Royal Army Medical Corps. Though this was a less strenuous job, it was also significantly less pleasant and so he again transferred to the Press Corps, which he found suited him far better.

He was in Cape Town in 1898 where he met Rudyard Kipling and was inspired to begin writing and publishing poetry and songs. His first collection of ballads, The Mission that Failed! and was enough of a success that in 1899 he paid his way out of the armed forces in order to turn to writing full time. His first work was as a war correspondent for Reuters who kept him in Africa to cover the Boer War, and then for the Daily Mail in 1900 and various other periodicals after that. It was while he was in South Africa that he met and married Ivy Maude Caldecott, who was 21 when they married in 1901, despite her Wesleyan missionary father's strong opposition to the union, for several reasons, one of which was that Wallace's writing was not turning quite the profit he had expected it would. War and Other Poems and Writ in Barracks, both published in 1900, had not proved as popular as his first collection. Eleanor Clare Hellier Wallace, their first child, died of meningitis in 1903 and, in rather deep debt, they returned to London. Wallace used his contacts with the Daily Mail to get work with them in London, electing to write detective novels as a means of making quick money.

Wallace met Polly, his birth mother, in 1903. He didn't remember her from his childhood as he had been too young when she became unable to visit, so it was as though they were meeting for the first time.

She was sixty years old and terminally ill, living in abject poverty. She had come to Wallace seeking financial support, but he turned her away. She died in the Bradford Infirmary later that year. In 1904 he and Ivy had a son, Bryan. He was still writing and had completed his first thriller, *The Four Just Men*. Since nobody would publish it he resorted to setting up his own publishing company which he called Tallis Press and he published a serialised version of *The Four Just Men* in 1905. He received promotional assistance from the Daily Mail in which he ran a competition for entrants to guess the method of murder in the final chapter, with a prize of £1,000 for a correct guess. Although the paper's proprietor, Lord Alfred Harmsworth, refused Wallace the £1,000 prize money, Wallace persisted and went ahead with the competition, recklessly advertising on billboards and buses all over the country, hoping to expand his advertisements across the Empire. His worried colleagues at the Daily Mail managed to convince him to lower the prize money to £500, split into a first prize of £250, a second prize of £200 and a third of £50, but with the total cost of his advertisements nearing £2,000 he would need to sell £2,500 worth of copies before he could see any profit. He was confident that this could be achieved in just three months.

Though he had remarkable enthusiasm, it became clear that his managerial skills left a lot to be desired. It soon emerged that nowhere in the competition terms and conditions had he included a clause limiting the competition to one single winner; instead, any entrant with a winning answer was entitled to their corresponding prize money. Thus, if ten entrants guessed the first prize answer, the competition was obliged to pay each entrant £250. This error was only noticed after the competition had been closed and the solution had been printed in the final installment of the novel, meaning that not only was there no opportunity to write his way out of enormous financial obligation, but the entrants who had guessed correctly would by now have read the final chapter and know they had done so. £250 was an enormous amount of money to the average Edwardian family and those entitled to it were likely to make a lot of noise if they didn't receive their money. Despite this, Wallace's fist instinct was to attempt to ignore the issue entirely, even as he discovered that he initial calculations had been dramatically over-enthusiastic and it would take nearer to two years of continuous sales to break even at the initial cost of £2,500, let alone the new figure which included every correct guesser. Compounding the problem even further was the awful realisation that as sales continued throughout the initial three month period and Wallace approached the £2,500 break-even figure, new readers were still eligible to enter and guess correctly. Though it is unknown how much he eventually owed his readers, Lord Harmsworth found himself having to loan over £5,000 in order to protect the reputation of the newspaper, since 1906 had come around and there still hadn't been a list printed of all prize-winners. It was less a charitable act than one of a man anxious that the failure would reflect ill on his own paper. Wallace filed for bankruptcy shortly thereafter and as a token gesture to his creditors sold the rights to the novel to Sir George Newnes, a publisher and editor, for £75. In the midst of this chaos though, Wallace managed to write and published *Smithy*, which would become the first of a series of *Smithy* novels.

Following this fiascos Wallace was dismissed from the Daily Mail in 1907 when inaccuracies which were found in his reporting, resulting in libel cases being brought against the paper. That year he became the first reporter to be fired from the Daily Mail and was his awful reputation prevented him from finding work at any other papers. Despite all this, though, he travelled to the Congo Free State later that year and reported on the criminal treatment of the Congolese people by King Leopold II of Belgium and the Belgian rubber companies. Up to fifteen million Congolese were killed in various atrocities, and Wallace was asked to serialise stories based on his experiences for her penny magazine *Weekly Tale-Teller*. He and Ivy had another daughter, named Patricia, in 1908. Though his new work for *Weekly Tale-Teller* was bringing in some money, their financial situation was still dire and Ivy was occasionally forced to sell off her jewellery and possessions in order to pay for food. In 1911 his Congolese stories were published in a collection called *Sanders of the River*, which quickly became a bestseller. He would publish eleven more such collections featuring a total of 102 stories of adventure and tribal life set on the river Congo.

From 1908 he started to enjoy a revival of both his success and his reputation. The majority of his initial writing he sold outright in order to make money as quickly as possible and placate his creditors in the United Kingdom and South Africa, but as his success saw the reestablishment of his reputation he began to find work once again as a journalist, beginning in horse racing for the *Week-End*, the *Evening News* and then as an editor for the *Week-End Racing Supplement*. Following this success he started his own racing papers, *Bibury's* and *R. E. Walton's Weekly*, eventually buying his own racehorses and losing thousands gambling. His success was insufficient to support his newly extravagant lifestyle and his marriage began to fail in the light of his financial irresponsibility. He and Ivy had their last child together, Michael Blair Wallace, in 1916, and she filed for divorce in 1918 moving to Tunbridge Wells with her children.

Wallace began to fall for his secretary Ethel Violet King and they married in 1921, having a child, Penelope Wallace, in 1923, who would herself go on to become a successful crime writer. Wallace now began to take his career as a fiction writer more seriously, signing with Hodder and Stoughton in 1921. He now began to organize his contracts more carefully, arranging for royalties and properly organized promotions, run by people more business-minded than himself. He was marketed as the 'King of Thrillers' and they gave him the trademark image of a trilby, a cigarette holder and a yellow Rolls Royce. He was truly prolific, capable not only of producing a 70,000 word novel in three days but of doing three novels in a row in such a manner. His publishers signed off on almost everything he wrote as soon as he turned it in, estimating that by 1928 one in four books being read at any time was written by Wallace, for alongside his famous thrillers he wrote variously in other genres, including but not limited to science fiction, non-fiction accounts of WWI which amounted to ten volumes and screen plays. Eventually he would reach the remarkable total of 170 novels, 18 stage plays and 957 short stories.

Wallace became chairman of the Press Club which to this day holds an annual Edgar Wallace Award, rewarding 'excellence in writing'. In 1923 he broadcasted a report on the Epsom Derby horse race for the British Broadcasting Company, making him the first ever radio sports correspondent. His ex-wife Ivy had suffered from breast cancer between 1923-1924, and it eventually killed her in 1926 despite a successful operation to remove a tumour the year before. He wrote the essay "The Canker in our Midst" in 1926 which dealt, aggressively and controversially, with the problem of paedophilia in show business, describing how children were unwittingly left open to sexual abuse, and linking paedophilia with homosexuality. Its tone has been described as "intolerant, blustering, kick-the-blighters-down-the-stairs". He was appointed chairman of the British Lion Film Corporation on the back of the success of *The Ringer* and on the agreement that he give British Lion first choice on all his future work. This contract gave him an annual salary and a large amount of stock with the company, along with a stipend on all British Lion production of his work and 10% of their annual profits. This extraordinary contract gave him annual earnings by 1929 of almost £50,000, or almost £2 million in 2014.

He now became an active figure in politics, entering the 1931 general election as a Liberal contestant in Blackpool, rejecting the current government in favour of free trade. He lost the election by over 33,000 votes and went to America in late 1931, once again deeply in debt after buying the *Sunday News* which closed six months later. In America he quickly found work as a script doctor for RKO Pictures, enjoying early success with the 1932 adaptation of *The Hound of the Baskervilles*. This success, along with that of the play *The Green Pack*, established his reputation in America and he was able to see his own work adapted for film, beginning with *The Four Just Men*. His most successful theatrical work, *On The Spot*, which explores the life of Al Capone, has been described as "arguably, in construction, dialogue, action, plot and resolution, still one of the finest and purest of 20th-century melodramas". These successes led to his assignation on RKO's "gorilla picture" which would become famous as King Kong in 1933.

He worked on the first draft though he was beginning to experience severe headaches which brought about a diagnosis of diabetes. Despite taking medication to address his condition, it deteriorated in a matter of days. His wife booked him passage home but soon heard that he had entered a coma and died of his condition and double pneumonia on the 7th of February 1932 in North Maple Drive, Beverly Hills. In his honour the bell at St. Bride's church on Fleet Street tolled for the duration of the morning while the flags flew at half-mast. He was buried near his home in England at Chalklands, Bourne End, in Buckinghamshire. Once again, at the time of his death he was in severe debt, mostly to racing bookkeepers, though these debts were settled within two years thanks to the enormous royalties his estate continued to receive from his contracts. His writing has been translated into 29 languages, and is considered one of the most important bodies of Colonial writing.

Edgar Wallace – A Concise Bibliography

African Novels
Sanders of the River (1911)
The People of the River (1911)
The River of Stars (1913)
Bosambo of the River (1914)
Bones (1915)
The Keepers of the King's Peace (1917)
Lieutenant Bones (1918)
Bones in London (1921)
Sandi the Kingmaker (1922)
Bones of the River (1923)
Sanders (1926)
Again Sanders (1928)

Four Just Men (Series)
The Four Just Men (1905)
The Council of Justice (1908)
The Just Men of Cordova (1917)
The Law of the Four Just Men (US title: Again the Three Just Men) (1921)
The Three Just Men (1926)
Again the Three Just Men (US title: The Law of the Three Just Men) (1929) a.k.a. Again the Three

Mr. J. G. Reeder (Series)
Room 13 (1924)
The Mind of Mr. J. G. Reeder (US title: The Murder Book of Mr. J. G. Reeder) (1925)
Terror Keep (1927)
Red Aces (1929)
The Guv'nor and Other Short Stories (US title: Mr. Reeder Returns) (1932)

Detective Sgt. (Inspector) Elk series

The Nine Bears or The Other Man or The Cheaters (1910)
revised as Silinski - Master Criminal (1930)
The Fellowship of the Frog (1925)
The Joker or The Colossus (1926)
The Twister (1928)
The India-Rubber Men (1929)
White Face (1930)

Educated Evans (Series)
Educated Evans (1924)
More Educated Evans (1926)
Good Evans (1927)

Smithy (Series)
Smithy (1905)
Smithy Abroad (1909)
Smithy and The Hun (1915)
Nobby or Smithy's Friend Nobby (1916)

Crime Novels
Angel Esquire (1908)
The Fourth Plague or Red Hand (1913)
Grey Timothy or Pallard the Punter (1913)
The Man Who Bought London (1915)
The Melody of Death (1915)
A Debt Discharged (1916)
The Tomb of T'Sin (1916)
The Secret House (1917)
The Clue of the Twisted Candle (1918)
Down under Donovan (1918)
The Man Who Knew (1918)
The Strange Lapses of Larry Loman (1918)
The Green Rust (1919)
Kate Plus Ten (1919)
The Daffodil Mystery or The Daffodil Murder (1920)
Jack O' Judgment (1920)
The Angel of Terror or The Destroying Angel (1922)
The Crimson Circle (1922)
Mr. Justice Maxwell or Take-A-Chance Anderson (1922)
The Valley of Ghosts (1922)
Captains of Souls (1923)
The Clue of the New Pin (1923)
The Green Archer (1923)
The Missing Million (1923)
The Dark Eyes of London or The Croakers (1924)
Double Dan or Diana of Kara-Kara (US Title) (1924)
The Face in the Night or The Diamond Men or The Ragged Princess (1924)
The Sinister Man (1924)

The Three Oak Mystery (1924)
The Blue Hand or Beyond Recall (1925)
The Daughters of the Night (1925)
The Gaunt Stranger or Police Work (1925) revised as The Ringer (1926)
A King by Night (1925)
The Strange Countess (1925)
The Avenger or The Hairy Arm (1926)
The Black Abbot (1926)
The Day of Uniting (1926)
The Door with Seven Locks (1926)
The Man from Morocco or Souls In Shadows or The Black (US Title) (1926)
The Million Dollar Story (1926)
The Northing Tramp or The Tramp (1926)
Penelope of the Polyantha (1926)
The Square Emerald or The Woman (1926)
The Terrible People or The Gallows' Hand (1926)
We Shall See! or The Gaol-Breakers (US Title) (1926)
The Yellow Snake or The Black Tenth (1926)
Big Foot (1927)
The Feathered Serpent or Inspector Wade or Inspector Wade and the Feathered Serpent (1927)
Flat 2 (1927)
The Forger or The Counterfeiter (1927)
Terror Keep (1927)
The Hand of Power or The Proud Sons of Ragusa (1927)
The Man Who Was Nobody (1927)
Number Six (1927)
The Squeaker or The Sign of the Leopard or The Squealer (US Title) (1927)
The Traitor's Gate (1927)
The Double (1928)
The Flying Squad (1928)
The Gunner or Gunman's Bluff (US Title) (1928)
Four Square Jane or The Fourth Square (1929)
The Golden Hades or Stamped In Gold or The Sinister Yellow Sign (1929)
The Green Ribbon (1929)
The Calendar (1930)
The Clue of the Silver Key or The Silver Key (1930)
The Lady of Ascot (1930)
The Devil Man or Sinister Street or Silver Steel
or The Life and Death of Charles Peace (1931)
The Man at the Carlton or The Mystery of Mary Grier (1931)
The Coat of Arms or The Arranways Mystery (1931)
On the Spot: Violence and Murder in Chicago (1931)
When the Gangs Came to London or Scotland Yard's Yankee Dick
or The Gangsters Come To London (1932)
The Frightened Lady or The Case of the Frightened Lady or Criminal At Large (1933)
The Green Pack (1933)
The Man Who Changed His Name (1935)
The Mouthpiece (1935)

Smoky Cell (1935)
The Table (1936)
Sanctuary Island (1936)

Other Novels
Captain Tatham of Tatham Island or Eve's Island or The Island of Galloping Gold (1909)
The Duke in the Suburbs (1909)
Private Selby (1912)
1925 - The Story of a Fatal Peace (1915)
Those Folk of Bulboro (1918)
The Book of all Power (1921)
Flying Fifty-five (1922)
The Books of Bart (1923)
Barbara on Her Own (1926)

Poetry Collections
The Mission That Failed (1898)
War and Other Poems (1900)
Writ In Barracks (1900)

Non-Fiction
Unofficial Despatches of the Anglo-Boer War (1901)
Famous Scottish Regiments (1914)
Field Marshal Sir John French (1914)
Heroes All: Gallant Deeds of the War (1914)
The Standard History of the War – Volumes 1 – 4 (1914)
Kitchener's Army and the Territorial Forces:
The Full Story of a Great Achievement (1915)
Vol. 2-4. War of the Nations (1915)
Vol. 5-7. War of the Nations (1916)
Vol. 8-9. War of the Nations (1917)
Famous Men and Battles of the British Empire (1917)
Tam of the Scouts (1918)
The Real Shell-Man: The Story of Chetwynd of Chilwell (1919)
People or Edgar Wallace by Himself (1926)
The Trial of Patrick Herbert Mahon (1928)
My Hollywood Diary (1932)

Screenplays
King Kong (1932, first draft of original screenplay, 110 pages) While the script was not used in its entirety, much of it was retained for the final screenplay.
The Hound of the Baskervilles (1932, British film)
The Squeaker (1930, British film)
Prince Gabby (1929, British film)
Mark of the Frog (1928, American film)
The Valley of Ghosts (192

Short Story Collections

The Admirable Carfew (1914)
The Adventure of Heine (1917)
Tam O' the Scouts (1918)
The Fighting Scouts (1919)
Chick (1923)
The Black Avons (1925)
The Brigand (1927)
The Mixer (1927)
This England (1927)
The Orator (1928)
The Thief in the Night (1928)
Elegant Edward (1928)
The Lone House Mystery and Other Stories (1929)
The Governor of Chi-Foo (1929)
Again the Ringer The Ringer Returns (US Title) (1929)
The Big Four or Crooks of Society (1929)
The Black or Blackmailers I Have Foiled (1929)
The Cat-Burglar (1929)
Circumstantial Evidence (1929)
Fighting Snub Reilly (1929)
For Information Received (1929)
Forty-Eight Short Stories (1929)
Planetoid 127 and The Sweizer Pump (1929)
The Ghost of Down Hill & The Queen of Sheba's Belt (1929)
The Iron Grip (1929)
The Lady of Little Hell (1929)
The Little Green Man (1929)
The Prison-Breakers (1929)
The Reporter (1929)
Killer Kay (1930)
Mrs William Jones and Bill (1930)
Forty Eight Short Stories (George Newnes Limited ca. 1930)
The Stretelli Case and Other Mystery Stories (1930)
The Terror (1930)
The Lady Called Nita (1930)
Sergeant Sir Peter or Sergeant Dunn, C.I.D. (1932)
The Scotland Yard Book of Edgar Wallace (1932)
The Steward (1932)
Nig-Nog and other humorous stories (1934)
The Last Adventure (1934)
The Woman From the East (1934) Co-written By Robert George Curtis
The Edgar Wallace Reader of Mystery and Adventure (1943)
The Undisclosed Client (1963)

Other
King Kong, with Draycott M. Dell, (1933), 28 October 1933 Cinema Weekly

Plays

An African Millionaire (1904)
The Forest of Happy Dreams (1910)
Dolly Cutting Herself (1911)
The Manager's Dream (1914)
M'Lady (1921)
Double Dan (1926)
The Mystery of room 45 (1926)
A Perfect Gentleman (1927)
The Terror (1927)
Traitors Gate (1927)
The Lad (1928)
The Man Who Changed His Name (1928)
The Squeaker (1928)
The Calendar (1929)
Persons Unknown (1929)
The Ringer (1929)
The Mouthpiece (1930)
On the Spot (1930)
Smoky Cell (1930)
The Squeaker (1930)
To Oblige A Lady (1930)
The Case of the Frightened Lady (1931)
The Old Man (1931)
The Green Pack (1932)
The Table (1932)

www.ingramcontent.com/pod-product-compliance
Lightning Source LLC
Chambersburg PA
CBHW061452170626
46811CB00004B/1484

* 9 7 8 1 7 8 7 8 0 0 3 3 5 *